He'd been around too long not to know that lightning could strike twice. That the one kiss they'd shared wasn't just some random fluke.

Kissing Kimi Taka—no matter how many times—was like lassoing lightning. Intoxicating, exhilarating and dangerous as hell.

Even knowing that, it took him too damn long to tear his mouth from hers, and when he did, he found his hands were wrapped around those long, silky skeins of dark hair. "Dammit to *hell*."

She pressed her lips together as if savoring the taste of him. Her voice was husky when she finally spoke. *"Sorry."*

Greg let out a strangled groan. "You're not really sorry?"

Kimi sucked in an audible breath. "No." Her fingers fluttered over the loosened knot of his tie. "Does it help if I take all responsibility? I kissed you. It is not as if you were an interested participant."

His gaze fastened on her face. "If you think I'm not interested, you haven't been paying attention."

Dear Reader,

I always find it a treat to participate in a multi-author continuity and this was certainly no exception. I so admire the talented authors who contributed to BACK IN BUSINESS—and wonder how I'm lucky enough to be among them!

What makes BACK IN BUSINESS particularly fun, too, is getting to revisit the characters I came to know so well in *Family Business*.

Kimi Taka was a somewhat mischievous child last time around; now she's a somewhat mischievous adult. Even I wondered at times how to control her! Fortunately, there was the very non-mischievous Greg Sherman around to help us both along the way. I like to think they complement each other in the best of ways.

I hope you enjoy getting down to business—particularly the romantic kind—with Kimi and Greg as much as I did!

All my best,

Allison Leigh

ALLISON LEIGH

THE BOSS'S CHRISTMAS PROPOSAL

Silhouette

SPECIAL EDITION®

Published by Silhouette Books

America's Publisher of Contemporary Romance

Special thanks and acknowledgment to Allison Leigh
for her contribution to the BACK IN BUSINESS miniseries.

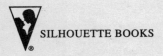

SILHOUETTE BOOKS

ISBN-13: 978-0-373-24940-4
ISBN-10:   0-373-24940-3

Recycling programs
for this product may
not exist in your area.

THE BOSS'S CHRISTMAS PROPOSAL

Visit Silhouette Books at www.eHarlequin.com

Printed in U.S.A.

ALLISON LEIGH

started early by writing a Halloween play that her grade-school class performed. Since then, though her tastes have changed, her love for reading has not. And her writing appetite simply grows more voracious by the day.

She has been a finalist for a RITA® Award and the Holt Medallion. But the true highlights of her day as a writer are when she receives word from a reader that they laughed, cried or lost a night of sleep while reading one of her books.

Born in Southern California, Allison has lived in several different cities in four different states. She has been, at one time or another, a cosmetologist, a computer programmer and a secretary. She has recently begun writing full-time after spending nearly a decade as an administrative assistant for a busy neighborhood church, and currently makes her home in Arizona with her family. She loves to hear from her readers, who can write to her at P.O. Box 40772, Mesa, AZ 85274-0772.

Once again, I owe my thanks to others for sharing with me some of their personal experiences with Japan.

Thank you, C.J., Brian and Karen.
The errors belong to me.

Thanks, also, to the fine authors
I had the privilege of working with on this series.

Not only were there some great laughs,
but I always learn something valuable along the way.

Lastly, to my very own Greg
(for whom Mr. Sherman was not named,
despite the rumors otherwise!) who makes it easy,
indeed, to write with some knowledge about the way
a man can hold a woman's heart.

Prologue

"You have decided to *what*?"

Kimiko Taka managed not to cringe at her father's very cool, very controlled question. Mori Taka rarely lost his temper, but she knew if he were going to, she would probably be the cause of it. A quick glance at her stepmother, Helen, told her that even she was looking somewhat distressed.

Kimi moistened her lips and tried not to look as nervous as she felt. "I have decided not to go back to school," she repeated.

Her father's eyes could not be a darker brown. She knew that, because when she looked in the mirror each morning, she saw that very same near-obsidian looking back at her. But at that moment, she felt quite certain that his eyes turned from brown to cold shards of jet.

"Is that so?" His tone became even milder. "Am I supposed to be more pleased by this decision of yours than I was when you last left school—because of expulsion? What do you plan to do with your time? Shop? Attend movie premieres with un-suitable escorts? Be photographed on topless beaches?"

Her hands curled. It had been *one* beach, and she had not been topless, exactly, but arguing the point would not earn her any points.

"Mori." Helen had been sitting next to Kimi's father since Kimi had entered the study of their lavish Chicago home. As always, Kimi's stepmother was the perfectly beautiful blond foil for her dark, powerfully built husband, and now she slid her slender hand over Mori's shoulder.

There had been a time—a time that Kimi could still remember—when her most intimidating father would not have allowed such familiarity. Not even from a loved one. More to the point, maybe, no one would have dared such familiarity.

Helen had changed all of that, though. She had changed Mori's life. And Kimi's. She was the only mother that Kimi had known, since her own had died when she was a baby.

"Perhaps we should let Kimi explain," Helen finished calmly. But the green gaze she focused on Kimi held a plea that the explanation had better be good.

Kimi managed not to wring her hands. The truth was, she hated worrying Helen just as much as she did her father. "I—I want to work for the corporation," she said, in more of a rush than she would have liked. She really, *really* hated feeling defensive.

Perhaps she had inherited that trait from her father.

His expression was inscrutable, though she detected a faint thinning of his lips.

She moistened her lips again. "I believe I will receive a more important education in the real world, Papa. My professors—" She broke off, aware that her father probably did not want to hear another rehashing of her low opinion of her professors.

What was it about even the most educated of individuals that they could be so preoccupied by a person's pedigree? Even when she had *tried* to fail a course, she had not been allowed to. Her professors had always found some reason to make allowances for her. Some reason to change a well-deserved failing grade into a passing one. Anything to honor the family name.

Mori was not looking any more convinced. Even the faintly encouraging expression on Helen's face was looking strained.

If Kimi were not careful, she was either going to start crying or stomp her foot with temper and prove that she was the child everyone believed her to be.

She rose from the couch facing her parents. "Everyone in this family has been able to contribute in some way to TAKA-Hanson. Everyone except me. I am asking for an opportunity. Let me start somewhere. I will learn. I will work hard."

"Like you worked hard at those mediocre grades you managed to earn?"

She winced. Mediocre indeed, but still passing, when she had intentionally tried to fail. "Working for the family business will be different. You have my promise. If I fail you—" she swallowed, thinking about the numerous times she had already done that "—or disgrace you, I will never ask for another favor."

Mori's lips compressed. His gaze flicked to his wife, then back to Kimi. She knew it had to be her imagination that there was a trace of humor in his eyes. Her father had very little reason to feel humorous where she was concerned, and she knew it. She knew that his reaction was deserved.

"I will follow whatever direction you set for me," she added, feeling decidedly desperate.

"Even if that means agreeing to a suitable marriage?"

She barely kept her jaw from dropping. She looked at Helen. "Um…"

"Mori," Helen chided softly. "You're beginning to sound like *your* father." Mori looked irritated, but Helen did not seem to let that bother her as she turned again to Kimi. "Perhaps Kimi should be given this opportunity. I'll find someplace for her in our new hospitality division. The Taka Kyoto still has openings."

Kimi's lips parted, but she managed to contain the protest that had immediately sprung to life. She was Japanese by birth. Had been raised in Japan for much of her childhood. But the United States was the country of her heart. She had rather hoped to stay here—maybe even be part of the Taka Chicago, which was scheduled to open the following year. She had *never* thought she would be shuttled off to Japan.

"What does Kimi know about hotels?" Mori asked, as if she were not even present. "Other than staying in one?"

She was glad he didn't add some caustic comment about the reasons she had supposedly been caught in some of those hotels.

Helen was ever positive, though. "She *was* studying business administration, Mori. Plus she's bright, she's capable and she's energetic. As she said, she can learn."

"She is a child."

"She is twenty-one," Kimi inserted, trying not to be too sarcastic, knowing that it would not help her cause.

Mori and Helen both looked back at her. "The development and opening of Taka Hotels has been a major undertaking," Helen said, her soft voice serious. "I—we've—courted the finest people in the world to bring it about. It's not a playground for you, darling."

"I am not looking for a playground."

"What *are* you looking for, Kimi-chan?"

Kimi eyed her father. She wanted to prove herself on her own merits. Just for once. "I want to be a credit to the Taka name." That was also true and probably more in line with her father's desires. "I believe I can do that better in the real world than I can in the academic one." The only proof she had been finding in school was that she was never treated impartially.

He made a low "hmm," clearly unconvinced.

But it was Helen who spoke. "I'll speak with our general manager in Kyoto. See if there's anything suitable."

Kimi curtailed the urge to leap across the cocktail table to hug her stepmother. Kyoto or not, at least it was a chance. "Thank you. I will not disappoint you."

But her inward grin faltered when her father pinned her with his hard gaze. "See that you do not, Kimiko. See that you do not."

Chapter One

"There's nothing like the smell of sawdust and paint in the morning, is there?"

Greg Sherman smiled faintly and looked past Shin Endo, his hand-picked director of security for the Taka Kyoto. "As long as the smell is gone before we open for guests." His practiced gaze traveled over the soaring lobby space. In just a few weeks' time, it would need to be a spotless showcase, fit for bearing the esteemed name of Taka, as it welcomed the celebrated and the wealthy into its comfort.

Right now, there was still concrete underfoot where wood floors would be inlaid among gleaming marble, the walls were bare of paint and paper, there was enough visible wiring that it looked as if rats had been at work and laborers and hotel staff were fairly crawling all over.

But beyond the chaos, Greg saw the order.

More importantly, he saw the future.

"Speaking of guests," Shin said. "When's the pampered heiress supposed to arrive?"

Greg absently flipped his hand down his silk tie and stepped around a pallet of shrink-wrapped banquet chairs. He caught the eye of Marco, one of his maintenance crew, and gestured at the pallet. "Get this moved down to storage."

"Right away, Mr. Sherman."

He didn't wait to see that Marco followed words with action. "Next Monday," he answered Shin. He continued walking through the mess toward the offices behind reception, Shin keeping stride. At thirty-five, the other man was three years older than Greg, and about a half-foot shorter.

As far as Greg was concerned, there wasn't a better man in the field and fortunately, Helen Taka-Hanson hadn't quibbled over the price that it had taken to lure Shin away from his previous employer. One thing Greg could say about his boss was that she was willing to pay for the best. She was also willing to put her own efforts into a project. Since she'd hired Greg to be the general manager of the Taka Kyoto, she'd proven to be hands-on while still managing to let Greg and his crew do the work they'd been hired to do without undue interference.

Until now.

"You think she'll actually show up for work?"

"Kimiko Taka?" Greg shrugged. "I wouldn't take bets on it. She's a kid." A wild child, from all reports, whose social activities were often regaled by the press. Greg still wasn't pleased that Helen had stuck him with her stepdaughter. "Officially, she'll only be Grace's very junior sales associate." Grace Ishida ran the sales and catering department, which had responsibility for everything from banquets to full-scale conventions and everything in between. "I doubt being a peon will appeal to the girl too much." At which time, Kimi Taka would surely take herself right back out of his hair.

"And Boss-lady agreed to that position for her stepdaughter?"

"She suggested it," Greg admitted. He understood Shin's surprise, considering he'd shared it. Helen could have ordered her stepdaughter to be put into a management position—no matter how unqualified the girl would have been—and he'd have been powerless to stop her. But Helen hadn't. She'd asked for entry level, and that was all.

So Greg would just have to tolerate Helen's small measure of interference. Given everything on his plate, it would be only a minor nuisance until the reputably spoiled Kimiko became bored and moved on to her next escapade. It couldn't come soon enough for him. The fewer hitches they had, the better he liked it.

Nothing was more important than proving he had what it took to helm this place.

And after this place...his own.

"Here." He handed over a thick, stapled report. "The latest guest list for the New Year's Eve gala."

Shin took the report, grimacing. "When are the computers supposed to be online?"

"Last week. Lyle Donahue's got his entire department working on it. You'll see that we'll need extra security for the event." The list contained not only the expected Hanson and Taka faces, but government officials, several celebrities from a half dozen countries and a handful of crowned royals.

Shin was perusing the pages. "You got it. Where's Bridget, anyway?" Bridget McElroy was Greg's secretary.

"Called in sick."

Shin's dark eyebrows rose a little. "That's a first." He turned to leave the office. "I'll get back to you on the numbers for the extra security."

Already turning his mind to the dozen other matters needing his attention, Greg barely heard him. With Bridget out and their computer network still dysfunctional, it was proving to be a trying day.

He grabbed the folder of items he still needed copied for the staff meeting he'd be holding in another hour and left the office. He'd take the materials down to Grace's office. She'd loan him a body who could put together the packets for him.

But he stopped short at the sight that met him.

The pallet of chairs was still sitting in the middle of the lobby floor. Almost eclipsing it, however, was a stack of luggage.

A growing stack of luggage, thanks to the diminutive female directing Marco and a half-dozen other eager helpers. "Please do be careful with that one." The luggage owner darted forward and took a small case from a guy who, ten minutes earlier, had been on a scaffold twenty feet off the ground painting trim work. "Rather fragile, you see." Her smile was impish.

The painter didn't look offended when she took the case. Probably too busy looking at the legs displayed between her over-the-knee white boots and one of the briefest skirts Greg had seen outside of a fashion runway.

All around them, it was as if everyone—the laborers, the staff—had decided it was time to stop whatever it was they were supposed to be doing so they could witness the moment.

The pampered heiress had arrived.

Early.

"Here." Shin appeared, pushing a luggage cart that Greg knew he'd had to retrieve from the mezzanine level, where they were all being stored until the hotel opened for guests. "This might be useful." He shot Greg an amused glance as he stopped beside Kimiko Taka.

The girl swept a slender, ivory hand over her shoulder, pushing aside her thick tumble of deep brown hair. She turned, not even needing to beckon before Marco hurried into action, deftly stacking her luggage onto the cart, and treated Greg to her rear view.

The hair—he'd seen it photographed in newspapers and gossip rags looking any number of ways from straight and nauseatingly pink, to black and rainwater slick—was now swirling down the back of her white fur jacket in a mass of ringlets that almost reached her waist. But it was the minuscule skirt beneath the hip-length jacket that damnably caught even Greg's attention.

Tasty.

The word was printed right across her derriere, outlined in sparkling pink stitching.

He felt a pain settle between his eyebrows. Taka hotels were all about taste. *Good* taste. "Ms. Taka."

The girl whirled on her impossibly high heels to face him. "Yes?"

"Dōzo yoroshiku." Despite his misgivings about her, he greeted her with the faint bow that had become automatic for him in the month since he'd been at the Taka. "I am Greg Sherman, the—"

"—the general manager here at the Taka," she finished in slightly accented English. "Yes. My parents speak most highly of you." Despite the fact that she was the Japanese-born one here, she eschewed the usual practice of returning his circum-spect bow and stuck out her hand instead in a thoroughly Western greeting. "How do you do?"

"You've taken us by surprise, actually." He clasped her hand briefly. Long enough to feel how slender her fingers were, how cool her hands were and how electricity shot up his arm at the contact. He released her and reached for the strap of the rescued case that she'd looped over her shoulder. "We didn't expect you until next week."

Her hand brushed against his again as she released the strap. Her deep brown eyes were sparkling. "Better early than late, surely?" In a smooth move, she slid her jacket off her shoulders to reveal a shimmering white, silk blouse through which a pink, lacy bra was plainly visible. Before she could toss the jacket on the mountain of geometrically stacked luggage, half a dozen hands reached out to catch it, earning a seemingly delighted little laugh from her. "In any case, this is quite a welcoming committee."

"Who have other matters to attend to," Greg said pointedly. Looking over her head was easy because, even with the stiletto-heeled boots, the top of those bouncing brown curls didn't reach his shoulder. He gave Marco a look, but the young man was evidently not ready to give up his impromptu bellman duty.

"I can take these to Ms. Taka's room," he offered.

Kimiko looked over at Marco. "Oh, would you mind?" She gave him a smile that could have melted a glacier. On Marco, it was devastating. Greg could practically see the maintenance worker dissolve into a puddle.

His annoyance deepened. "Focus that attention on the pallet, Marco. I expected it to be moved the first time I told you."

The young man flushed at the rebuke. "Sorry, Mr. Sherman." He moved from hoarding the gleaming-bronze luggage cart to the pallet jack. He ducked his chin as he maneuvered the pallet away from them. "Ms. Taka."

Kimi smiled gently at the remorseful man. For pity's sake, it was just a stack of chairs amid a thoroughly chaotic and un-finished hotel lobby. "It was very nice meeting you, Marco."

His smile was sudden and beaming. "You, too, Miss Taka." He pushed the contraption bearing several high stacks of chairs across the concrete.

The construction noise around her suddenly seemed loud, and Kimi sucked in a quick breath before turning back to Greg Sherman.

He did not look anywhere near as kind as the departing Marco. Even though she had done her research about the man in her few weeks before leaving Chicago, she was unaccount-ably nervous now that they were face-to-face.

Sadly, the black-and-white head shot that had accompanied his vitae in Helen's files had done little to prepare her for the real thing. The photo had only shown a severely conservative man with darkish hair and light eyes who looked as if he rarely smiled.

Helen had told Kimi that she had hand-picked Greg Sherman

to be the general manager of the Kyoto location, and Kimi had been surprised, because her stepmother usually liked people with a little more…life…to them.

But Greg Sherman, in the flesh, was definitely fuller of life than that bland photo had been. Oh, his hair *was* conservatively short, but the medium brown waves looked like they would escape over his brow given the least provocation. The deep brown suit he wore was well-tailored if not exactly cutting the edge of male fashion, but she supposed it was the ideal choice for a man helming a new first-class hotel.

Then there was the fact that just the brief graze of his hand had left her skin tingling.

She reminded herself that this was her boss. Nothing more. Nothing less.

"I am sorry to have caused a distraction," she said sincerely. "It is good to be here."

The light eyes of the photograph were actually a very distinctive, very pale shade of green. No bluish tinge. No hint of brown. Just a pale green surrounded by a defining black ring that made them all the more startling, and they were looking her over without a single hint of expression.

He did not even acknowledge her sentiment. Instead, he eyed the cart. "Is this all of your luggage?"

She was not certain if he had stressed the *all* or not. But she was absurdly grateful that she had decided to leave a few things back in Chicago, or there would have been more. Still, she might as well admit to the obvious. "I never did learn the art of packing light. And yes, this is all."

He did not return her smile. "Mrs. Taka-Hanson told me that you've asked to stay on-site. You'll want to settle in."

She would not lose her good humor just because the man had the personality of a plank of oak. A very tall, very broad in the shoulder plank of oak. "Yes, if only to get this stuff out of the lobby."

He seemed to let out a faint sigh. "If you wouldn't mind waiting, I'll get your room key."

Kimi looked past him to the wide, curving sweep of the reception desk. She imagined that beneath the thick plastic and protective paper covering nearly every surface, it would be as spectacular as the one at the Taka San Francisco. She had heard that things were a little behind here, but she had expected the hotel interior to look a little more...finished. "Is the rest of the hotel in such—" she hesitated for a moment, trying to find a suitable word that would not sound as if she were being judgmental.

"—chaos? Today seems somewhat more so than usual." For an infinitesimal second—so brief that she would later wonder if she had imagined it—his gaze dropped from her face to her toes, hitting all points in between. "Our computer network isn't operational yet," he added. "It adds a fresh dimension to the challenges our team's already facing."

The explanation was smooth. Almost smooth enough that she could brush away the idea that she was a contributing factor to his chaos. Almost.

So, Mr. Sherman figured he had her number, did he?

She swept away the sinking disappointment and lifted her chin a little, giving him the same kind of direct look that she had learned at her father's knee. "Well, I appreciate the opportunity to be here." She rested her hand on the cool bronze of the luggage cart and smiled with as much good humor and grace as she had learned from her stepmother. "As you can see, I come hoping to be prepared for anything."

He remained unimpressed. "Shin."

The slender man who had brought the luggage cart snapped to attention.

"Arrange for Ms. Taka's things to be taken up to the Mahogany Suite."

"Right away."

Kimi retrieved her jacket and draped it over her arm, smiling at the man as he guided the cart across the concrete, before it was handed off to two other younger men. She was not surprised. She recognized Shin Endo from his photo, too, and it seemed unlikely that the security director for Taka Kyoto would concern himself with bellman duties.

Speaking of which. She hurriedly fell into step behind Greg, who was striding toward the reception area. "Have all the staff positions been filled now?" Three weeks ago, when she had pretty much begged her father not to have her drawn and quartered for dropping out of school, the staff roster here had been only partially filled.

"No." His answer did not invite further inquiry and she did not know whether to be delighted or aggravated. Yes, she knew she was coming in at a very junior level. Helen had made that more than clear when she had told Kimi what she could expect once arriving in Kyoto. But did that mean he could not discuss even some basic matters with an interested staff member, junior or not?

He slapped a thick folder down on the long, curving desk and walked around where it very nearly met the opposite and inner curve of an open staircase. Even behind the chest-high reception desk, Greg looked ridiculously tall. More like an American quarterback than an urbane hotel manager. That detail also had not shown through Helen's black-and-white photo.

Kimi dropped her jacket onto the desk and the thick plastic covering the wood crinkled. "How many employees live here on-site?"

He did not look up from whatever it was he was focusing on behind the desk. "Not many. Will you need more than one key?"

For what? All the wild parties he assumed she would be having? She kept the thought to herself and smiled demurely when he looked up at her. "Not unless I lose it."

With a faint snap, he pushed a traditional brass key into a small padded portfolio. But when she expected him to hand it to her, he held on to the small square and rounded the desk again. Her tote containing the only items that Kimi considered truly essential—her laptop and her few framed family photographs—was still hanging from his shoulder. "If you'll come this way, I'll show you to your room." He extended his hand in a smooth, indicating gesture. "Our main elevators are through the lobby and beyond the fountain."

Aggravation was edging out delight. "I am sure you have more important things to do." He was treating her as if she were a guest. A not particularly welcomed one, at that. "I can find my way on my own."

"Not at all." Olympic ice-skating could have been performed on that deeply smooth voice.

Learning how to mimic Mori Taka's direct and intimidating stare was one thing. Maintaining it against those stained-glass eyes of Greg Sherman's was another.

She looked away, busying herself with the jacket and sailed across the lobby passing what she assumed would be the fountain once it received the advent of water. Greg still beat her to the elevator bank, his long stride easily eclipsing hers. He pressed the call button and the wood-paneled doors of the nearest car opened.

She stepped inside. The floor of the elevator was carpeted in a taupe, tonal stripe that still smelled new. He pressed the button for the twenty-first floor and the doors sighed closed. Kimi knew that she was successful in keeping a pleasant expression on her face, because she could see their faint reflections in the mottled, mirrored interior.

Above the elevator doors, a beautiful, old-fashioned clock face showed the progress of their ascent. Unfortunately, that progress seemed dauntingly slow. If he were any other hotel manager, he would have been falling over himself to please her.

That was something she was not interested in, she reminded herself. She was here to work, not to be fawned over. She had had enough of that at college.

"Is there someone in particular I should see about my duties?"

"Human Resources is located on the lower level. I'll tell them to expect you in the morning."

That had not exactly answered her question. She rather doubted it was because he was unaware of the particular details of her assignment there. But she did not question him further. Her gaze rose to the floor indicator again. One floor to go.

She tucked her hair behind her ear. She probably should not have spent the morning before shopping in New York with a friend. Lana Sheffield was a friend from years ago who now worked for a fashion magazine. But she had her eye on being a designer, and Kimi had gone along with being Lana's "practice" project. As a result, Kimi had stepped onto the plane in New York—having nearly missed the flight in the first place—looking exactly the way she had looked after Lana had finished having her fun.

Kimi had spent more than half a day in the air, trying to sleep and mostly failing. Now here in Kyoto, the workday was nearly done. She had never enjoyed the time difference between Japan and the States. It always left her feeling dim.

The elevator slid to a seamless halt, emitting a soft, mellow chime the moment before the doors opened. She stepped past her new boss onto more new carpet—champagne-colored this time and stretching across the wide corridor so perfectly it looked as if no human foot had ever trod on it. This level was as beautifully finished as the lobby was decidedly unfinished. She wondered if the twenty-second floor—the top floor—was finished, as well.

"At the end on your right." Greg's voice seemed even deeper there in the hushed silence.

Kimi headed down the hall, looking curiously at the spaciously separated guest-room doors they passed. All were closed. The room numbers were displayed on small metal origami sculptures affixed to the wall beside each door. She had no way of knowing for certain if any of the rooms were occupied. Given the state of the lobby, she did not imagine that they were, but who knew? Maybe Greg's room was on this floor, too.

A faint shiver drifted down her spine at the thought.

Dread or excitement? A draft, she thought, quelling the debate inside her head.

He had reached the door ahead of her and unlocked it. "We've been using this suite for some advance photos, which is why it has a lock at all. The access control won't be activated until later next week. After we'd expected you." He gave her a glance.

She refused to apologize again for being early. So she just kept her smile in place.

A smile he did not return. "You'll be issued a key card at that point. Until then, you'll have to use the old-fashioned method." He tucked the metal door key into the portfolio and handed it to her as he pushed open the door and waited for her to enter. "Security monitors for the suite will be up next week, also. The phones are operational now, of course," he said, following her through the short foyer to where the suite opened up into a gloriously spacious living area.

She could appreciate why the space had been used for photos. It was magnificently appointed.

He set her tote bag on the spotless surface of a mahogany dining-room table, complete with eight chairs upholstered in a beautiful deep sienna silk. "You have three lines. More can be arranged if necessary. Wireless internet is available here in your suite and throughout the facility." He waved at the beautifully polished desk. "Printer and fax machine are located behind the drawer on the lower right. It slides out." He crossed to the bank of windows and drew open the bronze-colored silk drapes, leaving the pale oyster translucent sheers beneath in place. She could not tell for certain, but she suspected the view beyond would be as lovely as the view inside.

"Three of our five restaurants are already open on a limited basis," he continued blandly. "But Chef Lorenzo will make certain that all of your needs are met, no matter the time of day. The spa isn't yet open, but it, too, will be available for use in the next week."

"I'm here to work, not idle away my time in a spa."

He lifted an eyebrow and continued as if she hadn't spoken at all. "You can access the fitness center now, if you're not bothered by the interior finishing that's still being done. Otherwise, Michel St. Jacques—our concierge—can arrange any services you desire with another establishment."

He was not finished, though, as he introduced her to the individually controlled climate systems—one for the living area, one each for the two bedrooms and the three bathrooms—and showed her how to operate the safe hidden inside the walk-in dressing room, how to program the plasma televisions and on and on.

Kimi heard his smooth spiel but did not listen.

How could she, when her temper was rumbling inside her ears? She was not a guest.

But at last he finished extolling the virtues of the Mahogany Suite.

She was somewhat surprised that he did not actually say he hoped she enjoyed her stay at the Taka Kyoto as he ended near the door once more.

She gave him a practiced smile—the one that she had learned how to use when she was barely a teenager to combat the shyness that had plagued her—and slid a folded bill into his hand even as she opened the door herself for his exit. "Thank you so much, Mr. Sherman. I am sure I will be very comfortable."

Then, because it pleased her immensely to see the discomfited surprise cross his unrelentingly handsome face as he realized he had just been *tipped*, she closed the door on him.

Chapter Two

"She actually tipped you?" Shin was laughing at Greg as they watched a mattress delivery at the loading dock a short while later. "Was she generous, at least?"

Greg held up the U.S. currency between two fingers. Benjamin Franklin's face peered out from the folded hundred.

Shin just laughed harder.

Greg shoved the bill back into his pocket and rolled his shoulders against the itchy irritation that had tightened them from the moment he'd seen the pampered heiress's "tasty" behind.

He scratched his name on the paperwork the truck driver presented him and handed back the clipboard, already turning away. Shin kept pace, and they entered the echoing, vast exhibition space that occupied most of the lowest level of the hotel. In comparison to the rest of the establishment, the space, which was thankfully finished, looked almost industrial. Greg knew, however, the magic that could be done with the concrete and metal. All it took was imagination. And come the beginning of the year, the space was steadily booked for nearly two years out with everything from luxury automobile shows to wine auctions.

They went up the rear service stairs to the next floor where the bulk of the hotel offices were located. Concrete gave way to carpet, metal was replaced by wood. Even the staff who worked within the walls of the Taka were treated to excellent conditions. He'd managed a number of houses in his career, and he could truthfully say that wasn't always the case. For some hoteliers, the only thing that mattered was the front-end appearance. But Taka was first-class from front to back, bottom to top.

When Greg made a success of this hotel, he'd be able to command any position anywhere he chose. Gone would be the days of never feeling quite part of the exclusive world in which he lived and worked.

But first, he had to get *this* hotel operational. So far, there'd been more than a few setbacks. By the time Helen had brought him on board little more than a month ago, he'd definitely had his work cut out for him.

"Don't spend all that Franklin in one place," Shin said before disappearing into his office as they passed it. "I might want to win it at poker Friday night. Unless you're going to blow us off again to see Sondra Fleming."

"I'll be at the game," Greg assured drily. "So keep on dreaming about the hundred."

"Cards beating out the charms of the lady lawyer?"

He'd met Sondra shortly after arriving in Kyoto. They'd shared some entertaining time, but that was as far as it went. "She's looking for serious."

Shin grinned. "And you don't do serious."

"Only when it comes to work, my friend." Greg continued on until he reached Sales and Catering where he found Grace in her office, frowning over the table linens draped over her conference table. "What's wrong now?"

She pushed her hands through the long, blond hair that was courtesy of her Swedish mother. "Obviously, the color."

He eyed the linens. "They're red."

She sighed mightily. "In all the years I've known you, you'd think that by now you would have learned the difference between scarlet and red."

"*I* don't need to know the difference. You do. That's why I stole you from that shack in Tokyo."

She smiled. That "shack" was one of the most famous, premier hotels in all the world. "And I came because you *do* amuse me. This," she flipped out a napkin and dropped it atop the cloth already spread on the table, "is scarlet silk damask."

He could barely discern the difference between the two. "And that is what the others are supposed to be?"

"Exactly. We're using scarlet silk when we host the luncheon next week for the mayor, not red linen. At this rate, I'm going to have to make a trip I don't have time to make to Tokyo to beg, borrow and steal the *right* linens."

As far as he was concerned, the red ought to be fine. But he knew better than to step into Grace's decisions. Her acumen couldn't be topped. If she needed scarlet-colored whatever for some reason, then she needed it. "You've got staff," he reminded. "Send them on the hunt for you."

"Speaking of staff, Tanya did your packets. She's already taken them up to the training room."

"Thanks. Incidentally, you'll have one more soul to boss around tomorrow. If it's capable of being bossed."

Grace leaned back against her desk, crossing her arms. "Kimiko Taka's in the house. I heard."

Not surprising, since the only thing that ran more swiftly than gossip in a hotel was the water in the pipes. "Send her on your scarlet-colored errand," he advised, not entirely joking. "Rumor has it that shopping is one area where she really shines."

Grace's phone rang, and she picked it up, waving him out

of her office. He gave a tap on the oversized wall clock she'd hung alongside an enormous project board, reminding her to keep track of the time, before he left. He didn't want anyone missing this meeting. They had too much business to cover in too little time as it was.

He rounded the corner that would lead him back to his primary office—not the one located on the lobby level behind reception—and stopped short at the sight of Kimiko Taka exiting the elevator. She looked right then left, and spotted him.

If he wasn't mistaken, the high heel of her boot actually moved back a few inches. But that hesitation was brief before she strode straight for him. She didn't look quite like a runway model—for one thing, she was far too short. But she definitely had all of the attitude.

She stopped a good yard away from him. "Would you mind pointing me toward Human Resources?"

He touched the discreet bronze plaque hanging on the wall beside them on which the locations for the various departments were inscribed. "Go right at the end of this corridor."

An unexpected hint of pink rose in her cheeks, but her wide-set gaze didn't falter from his. In that, he had to give her credit. The girl knew how to look a person dead-on.

"Thank you." She stepped sideways, veering around him.

"Ms. Taka."

She stopped, slowly turning around to face him. "Yes?"

Her dark gaze followed his hand as he pulled the hundred-dollar bill from his pocket and the pink in her cheeks became even brighter. She brushed those pinup-girl ringlets off her shoulder again. "I suppose I should apologize."

Supposing and actually *doing* were two different things, but he had no interest in debating the point. He held out the folded bill and after a brief hesitation, she reached out to take it.

But he didn't release it. "The next time I see you on the

premises in a staff-related capacity, I expect you to dress appropriately."

"Yes—" she tugged harder on the bill "—sir."

"And by appropriate, I mean by *my* standards. Presumably one of those two dozen pieces of luggage that you brought contains a skirt longer than four inches and a blouse that buttons above your cleavage?" A surprisingly full cleavage, hugged by pink lace.

He jerked his gaze upward, realizing he was nearly staring.

Her glossy lips had compressed, and her long lashes had swept down. But when she spoke again, there was no hint of temper in her lilting voice. "Mr. Sherman, I can look like a nun if you'd like."

Even a full-scale nun's habit wouldn't dim the girl's undeniable beauty. The fact that he recognized that beauty wasn't bothersome.

What *was* aggravating was his damnable response to it. He was too old to be going dry-mouthed around a woman. Particularly the boss's daughter.

He released the bill. "Exercise some judgment, Ms. Taka. That's all I ask."

"Of course." Her lips stretched into a smile he was positive she didn't mean as she slipped the folded bill down into that cleavage. "Is there anything else, sir?"

He could have told her that the HR office was empty. He *should* have. But that smile, that *sir,* got under his skin. "No."

She lifted her chin and turned around again, striding to the end of the hall.

His teeth clenched when he realized he was watching the faint sway of *Tasty* until she turned out of sight.

He went into his office and shut the door. The last thing he needed was to see Kimiko Taka strutting her way back to the elevator once she discovered that every person in Human Resources had already left for the staff meeting.

* * *

Insufferable man.

Walking away from Mr. Plank-o'-Wood, it was all Kimi could do not to tug self-consciously at her skirt. That *was* more than four inches long, thank you very much. It reached a very respectable length, in fact, hitting her midthigh.

She could practically feel his gaze burning a hole in her spine before she reached the end of the hallway and turned out of his sight. Only then did she let herself exhale shakily. So much for the pep talk she had given herself twenty-some floors up in her suite.

She wanted to kick herself for not changing her clothes. But the truth was, she was so dog-tired that she had been afraid if she slowed down enough to change, she would just collapse in a heap.

Before finding her way to this lower level, all she had taken time to do was send a few text messages back home to let everyone know of her safe arrival and hook up her computer to transmit the Economics paper she had finished writing during the flight.

She may have dropped out of school to her parents' dismay, but that didn't mean after she had done so that she had not recognized the prudence of obtaining her degree anyway.

She had wanted just to do it on her own terms. In her own way. Finishing the classes online was a lot more tolerable to her than endless study groups and crowded lecture halls. It had even been worth having to prevail upon the dean's good graces where the Taka family name was concerned to be quietly reinstated.

None of which would matter a bit to Greg Sherman.

He was overreacting where her clothing was concerned anyway. The hotel was not yet open for guests, and the only people she had encountered were other employees.

Like her.

For now, though, the reminder that she *was* an employee— for the very first time in her life—was enough to have excitement dissolving her irritation, and she quickened her pace along the empty, carpeted corridor until she found the Human Resources department. It, too, was marked by a tastefully engraved metal sign, and she pushed through the double doors, entering a small lobby furnished with a half dozen chairs and a glass-topped reception desk.

All unoccupied.

"Hello?" She peered down the hallway behind the desk, but heard no response.

More unfilled staff positions?

She wondered if Helen knew just how bare some of the holes were here, but Kimi supposed she must. According to everything Kimi had learned, Helen and her father were satisfied that after a rocky beginning plagued by financial misdealings and construction delays, the hotel was firmly back on course under the guiding hands of Greg Sherman and continuing on its path to the height of its class.

She walked around the desk and down the hall, glancing in the half dozen offices that opened off of it. "Hello?" She reached the last office door. Closed and locked.

She exhaled and turned on her heel, striding out of the empty suite.

Greg *could* have told her that she was wasting her time. Probably the man needed to have some sort of amusements, though she found it hard to believe he had ever cracked a real smile.

She returned to the elevator but grew impatient when the call button she pressed remained lit and the doors remained closed. She could hear the faint swoosh of the car moving in the shaft, but it never seemed to make it far enough to stop there at the basement level. She tapped her toe and watched the minute hand on her wristwatch slowly move and then nearly jumped out of her skin when she heard a soft footfall behind her.

"Might as well take the service stairs, my dear. That

elevator's already busy running back and forth to the fifth."
A tall Nordic blonde wearing a deep blue running suit approached. "That's where the training room is, and that's where all the staff is supposed to be as of five minutes ago for a staff meeting. Grace Ishida." The woman stuck out her hand. "Director of Sales and Catering. And you must be Kimiko Taka."

"Yes, but make it Kimi, please." She shook the older woman's hand.

Grace was nodding. She pulled a folded piece of fabric out of her pocket. "Tell me. What color is this?"

She hesitated for a moment, feeling abruptly in the middle of a pop quiz. "Scarlet."

The other woman's eyes narrowed. "Not just a simple red?"

"I think it has too much orange in it to be a true red."

"Yes. It does." The fabric disappeared back in Grace's pocket, and looking satisfied, the other woman gestured Kimi past the unresponsive elevator. "You were born in Japan, weren't you?"

"Yes. I lived mostly in Tokyo until I was a teenager." Around another corner, and through a doorway, they entered the stairwell. Kimi had to nearly jog to keep up with the woman's long legs. The stairwell echoed with the sound of Grace's athletic shoes and Kimi's thin heels as they hurried up the steps. "But even before we moved there, I was enthralled with the United States."

"And now you're back in Japan."

Kimi managed a noncommittal agreement. She was there, yes, but not entirely by choice. It was just where her parents were allowing her to sink or swim.

Once they realized that she was not going under, she fully intended on returning to the country she loved.

They reached the main level, and Grace pulled open the door there, letting them out into another hallway, through which she led a circuitous way to the lobby. In comparison to the busyness there when Kimi had arrived, now the soaring, unfinished space was eerily silent. Fortunately, the bank of elevators beyond the dry fountain were responsive, a door opening the moment Grace called for it.

Inside, Grace leaned against the wall and studied Kimi. "Were you downstairs to look for Mr. Sherman?"

Kimi had seen Mr. Sherman, who had knowingly sent her on a wild goose chase. Seemingly, she imagined, to keep her away from his sanctified staff meeting. "I was trying to check in with Human Resources. I arrived earlier than they were expecting, but I thought it would be good to get started right away."

"We need all the hands we can get," Grace agreed. "But you found everyone already had gone. Hate it when that happens, don't you?" The melodious chime sounded and they left the elevator. "I assume you haven't had a proper tour of our facilities, yet? No. Well, through there is where the fitness center and the spa are located." She pointed toward the smoked-glass doors that blocked off the elevator banks. "There's also one of the indoor pools. It will be open for all guests of the hotel, whereas the pool that's up on seventeen has an age restriction of sixteen years and up. This way, though, are our training rooms." She headed in the opposite direction through a hidden doorway that was indistinguishable from the wooden-paneled wall around it. "Ordinarily, staff would only use the service elevators for access, of course. But there's no harm in using the main elevators for today. There are several floors in the hotel that are not available to the guest elevators at all, of course. The engine floors, laundry, et cetera. Before long, you'll have it all down pat."

Kimi was not so sure. Yes, she knew there were hundreds of things that went on behind the scenes of a hotel. She had just never before been part of it.

Their footsteps were silent on the carpet as they approached the opened entrance to the training room through which Kimi could see the backs of dozens of people already sitting at the narrow rows of tables facing the front of the room.

Facing Greg Sherman, who was witnessing their noticeably tardy arrival.

His gaze barely paused on Kimi and Grace as he continued speaking to the crowd, his deep voice easily carrying throughout the large room.

There were a few empty chairs there at the back of the room, and Kimi slipped into one as silently as possible while Grace headed toward the front of the room to take up a standing position near Shin Endo and another man whose face Kimi did not recognize from her research in Helen's files. A ponytailed Asian girl sitting to Kimi's right was busy taking notes in a three-ring binder. To Kimi's left, a dark-skinned young man was holding a microcassette recorder.

For a moment, she felt as if she were back in a lecture hall where every student was focused on the professor who could make or break their academic career with a swipe of his red pen.

"You've all been issued your security codes," Greg was saying. "Beginning Monday morning, you'll be required to use them when entering or leaving through the staff entrance. Some of you who've been here longer than a week have had plenty of time getting used to moving around without them. As of now, that ends." His gaze settled on Kimi's face as the order was met with a few groans. "The crews working on the lobby interior are being stepped up. Our first guests arrive December 15. That's fourteen days, people."

His gaze moved on, touching on nearly everyone and disproving her suspicion that he had been singling her out. "That's not a lot of time, and it will take all of us working together to ensure that when those guests do arrive, they're welcomed with every bit of luxury and excellence we want them to expect from the Taka brand. If you have a concern or a problem, you take it to your manager or to me. Remember that a hotel staff is a family. What happens in one department matters to all departments."

Kimi glanced around. Unless they were busy scribbling notes on the stapled packets that were at each seat, or on something else, the employees sitting at the narrow tables were giving Greg their rapt attention. Even she had to admit there was something mesmerizing about the way he spoke to them; as if they were all part of the conversation, rather than merely observant listeners.

He went on, talking about upcoming training schedules and staff rotations and project meetings.

Kimi leaned closer to the ponytail. "Do you have a spare pen?"

Without taking her pinpointed attention away from Greg, the girl pulled a dark gold ballpoint pen printed with a navy-blue TAKA logo on it and slid it to Kimi.

"Thank you," she whispered. She quickly jotted down the points that Greg was making on the back side of the packet in front of her and had started on another page before he turned the meeting over to Shin, who gave them an update on the closed-circuit security system.

"Our main concern is, of course, guest security," the man said. "We're not trying to police people's normal behavior. But we will act when there's a situation that seems to be developing. All points of entry and exit, the guest corridors and elevators, reception, will be on the circuit, which a team of security specialists will be monitoring 24/7. So any of you planning to catch a forbidden smoke outside on a fire escape be warned." He looked around the room, his expression seeming far too good-natured for the tough-as-nails expert he was reputed to be. "You'll be caught, and we'll have your walking papers ready before you blow out your light." There was a twittering of laughter around the room.

Kimi watched Greg to see if he showed some amusement. Of course, he did not. Then, as if he had sensed her attention, he looked her way again. She felt her cheeks warm and hurriedly focused on her notes. Through sheer effort she refrained from looking at him again for the rest of the hour-long meeting.

When the meeting concluded, a dozen of the women who had watched him adoringly throughout the meeting leapt from their seats to surround him with questions.

She hid a smile at the idea that he had his very own set of hotel groupies and returned the pen to the ponytail—Sue, according to the distinctive, engraved name badge the girl wore. "I'm Kimi. Are you from Kyoto?"

Sue shook her head. "San Francisco. From what I understand, there are only a few working here who *are* from Kyoto. The head of Housekeeping and a few men in Maintenance, I think. Other than that, we're sort of a United Nations when it comes to ethnicities of the staff."

"It's quite a leap from San Francisco to Kyoto."

"Not really. I started out at Taka San Francisco when it opened earlier this year but transferred here when I found out that *he* was the GM here."

Kimi glanced toward the "he" in question. Still surrounded by groupies. "You came to Japan because of Gr—Mr. Sherman?"

Sue didn't seem to see a single thing odd in that. "Of course." She closed her binder and stood. Around them, those that were not clamoring for Greg Sherman's attention were filing out of the room. "I'll be in reception once we open, but for now am working in reservations. You?"

"I don't yet know, actually." Helen had not offered that much detail. She would have, if she had known exactly what position Kimi would be filling.

"What hotel do you come from?"

"Well, none," Kimi admitted with a smile. "This is my first assignment in a hotel."

Sue's finely drawn eyebrows rose. "It's Mr. Sherman's policy that all staff members have at least three years' previous experience in a first-class hotel. You must have been born under a lucky star."

"I don't know about luck," she demurred, inching toward the door. Her stomach was growling and her head was pounding from lack of sleep. "It was nice meeting you, Sue. I am sure I will see you around."

"Maybe you'll be in reception." The other girl smiled. "They expect pretty women at the front desk."

Somehow, Kimi doubted that Greg Sherman intended for her to be registering guests. More likely, he would stick her in a housekeeping uniform and arm her with rubber gloves and a toilet brush for having the audacity of wanting to work there at all.

"Ms. Taka."

She wanted to groan when he spoke her name. Already she was coming to expect that not-quite-identifiable tone in Greg's voice when he addressed her.

Longing thoughts of the wide bed in her suite were swept aside, replaced by the reminder that he had deliberately withheld from her the fact that he had even scheduled this meeting.

She looked over at him. "Yes?"

Sue was giving her a reassessing look. "Oh. It was *that* star." The open, friendly expression on her face was gone. In its place was that odd combination of deference and suspicious fascination that Kimi had come to recognize when people discovered she was a Taka. Before she could respond, Sue quickly excused herself and disappeared out the door along with the dispatched groupies.

The only other people remaining in the training room were Grace Ishida, Shin Endo and a few others, who had their heads bent in quiet discussion at the head of the room.

Greg stopped in front of her. "Do you intend to disregard my authority at every turn?"

Her lips parted, insult digging through her. "Do you intend to exclude me from all staff functions?"

"You're not officially *on* the staff until you've completed your paperwork with Human Resources."

"Which I thought I would be doing until I discovered you had directed me to a completely unoccupied—" she realized her voice had risen, and hurriedly lowered it again "—an unoccupied department. If you had intended for me to learn about the staff meeting, you would have told me so yourself. You had plenty of opportunity, after all, but you would rather instruct me on the finer points of a television remote control. I am here to work, Mr. Sherman, and I would like the opportunity to be allowed to do so. Despite your obvious belief otherwise, I am not incompetent."

Annoyance tightened the already hard line of his jaw. "My apologies if it seemed that I implied any such thing. My point is merely that your presence here will be distracting enough without you looking—" his gaze raked down her body, scorching her skin "—like this. If you felt such compulsion to attend this meeting, you could have taken the time to change out of this unsuitable getup."

She was overtired. That was the only reason there was a deep sting behind her eyes. Yes, her outfit was somewhat less than conservative, but she was hardly dressed like a prostitute. Nevertheless, she could eat crow if she had to. She had already gotten plenty of practice while getting herself reinstated with the university, after all.

She made herself dip her head in a slight bow. "An error in my judgment for which I apologize. I thought it better not to be any tardier than I already was." She pressed her lips together for a moment and swallowed the constriction in her throat. "I am not here to be a distraction to anyone. I am here to be part of Taka Kyoto." How had he put it? "To be part of the family."

His slashing eyebrows quirked together over his blade-sharp nose. "And therein rests the problem, Ms. Taka. You're part of *the* family. Do you really think that anyone within these walls is ever going to be able to forget that?"

Kimi brushed the palms of her cold hands down the sleeves of her blouse. Disappointment coursed through her, sharp and deep. "I had hoped so, Mr. Sherman," she finally admitted huskily. "But that does not mean that I will tuck my tail and run back home to Mommy and Daddy. As I said, I am here to work. Once I begin, if you find me so unsatisfactory, you will undoubtedly treat *me* to a set of those walking papers Mr. Endo was talking about. But I am not walking away before I have even begun."

With her words still settling around them, she turned and *did* walk away because there was another thing she had learned from Helen. And that was the graceful art of making an exit.

Helen had just never warned Kimi that after said exit, a woman had to lean against a wall where she would not be seen, so her knees could stop shaking.

Chapter Three

"No, Bridget, don't worry about it. Last thing we need is a flu bug being spread around the hotel. Stay home, and take care of yourself." Greg disconnected the call and stared at the mess that had accumulated in only one day without his assistant.

God knew what shape the desk would be in by the time Bridget recovered.

He exhaled roughly and picked up the hotel phone to dial Human Resources. They'd have to assign someone temporarily since it now appeared that Bridget would, at the very least, be away for several days. "I need a body who can manage to answer basic correspondence and can keep me on schedule without requiring my constant babysitting," he told the girl who answered. "And I need them immediately."

"We'll send someone over to your office right away, sir."

"Thank you—" What was the girl's name? She'd come on board yesterday. Before Kimiko had set her sexy booted toe on the property. He grimaced. Focused harder. A redhead from Australia. "—Sheila." He nearly pounced on the name, feeling oddly victorious.

"My pleasure, sir."

He hung up again and went into the bathroom adjoining his office to finish shaving, which he'd been doing before Bridget's call interrupted him. Then he grabbed a fresh tie from the spares he kept in the closet and flipped it around the collar of his unfastened shirt. If he hadn't spent the entire night working in his office, he'd be taking care of these matters in his room.

From the small television in his office he listened to the international news. His phone buzzed again, and because he had no Bridget and no fill-in for her yet, he went out to answer it. "Sherman."

"Don't you sound so intimidating, honey." The female voice was bright and cheerful and sounded as if she were right next door rather than back in Berkeley, California, where his mother lived in the house he'd bought her two years earlier. "How's my little boy?"

He hit the speaker button and turned down the volume on the television. "All grown up, Mona." Which was more than he could say for his mother. "What's wrong?"

She laughed a little too heartily for a little too long. "Nothing has to be wrong for me to call my son."

Theoretically that was true, Greg knew, but experience told a different tale. "Okay, so how are you? You're taking your blood pressure medicine like you're supposed to?" He started buttoning up his shirt.

Through the speaker her exaggerated sigh sounded even more false. "I'm fine. Actually, I have good news."

He paused. Looked at the phone warily. "Oh?"

"Now, don't go sounding like that," she warned in a rush. "I'm just going on a little vacation, and I wanted to let you know so you wouldn't call and worry when I wasn't home. Europe!

Isn't that the most exciting thing? You know how much trouble it was last year to get my passport—my goodness, it never would have come through if not for you—and now I'm getting to use it."

The passport had been needed because she'd insisted on visiting him in Düsseldorf, where he'd been managing an aging grande dame of a hotel. But once there, she'd hated Germany and had flown home early. He hadn't been sorry to see her go. She was his mother, and he wanted her well. But close they were not.

He flipped up his collar and worked on the last two buttons. "Where in Europe?"

"Oh, we'll go where the spirit moves us."

He sat down on the corner of his desk. "We?" he prompted cautiously.

"I'm not very likely to go alone, am I?"

He rolled his head around on his suddenly tight neck. "Who is he?"

"Who says it's a he?"

Because it always was. He kept the thought to himself and waited. Fortunately, it didn't take long. His mother was a flighty creature who couldn't keep two cents in her pocket at any one time, but she was at least pretty honest about it.

"His name is Ralph," she finally said in a rush. "Can you believe that I've fallen in love with a man named *Ralph*? Now, don't get me wrong. It's a perfectly fine name, just a hair old-fashioned. Which is a good description of him, you know. Old-fashioned, I mean. We met at the grocery store. He caught my grapefruit. They'd dropped through the bottom of my bag. He rescued my fruit and then, oh, honey, he just rescued my heart. What can I say?"

Greg pinched the bridge of his nose. "When is this vacation supposed to occur? What about your job?" Her latest was as a clerk in a bookstore. Not that she needed the money, considering that Greg had been supporting her for years. But her history had proven that when she *was* working, Mona had a much easier time staying clean and sober. "You haven't been there long enough to merit vacation time."

"Oh, them," she dismissed airily. "Stuffed shirts. I should have known it when they told me what to wear to work."

His brain flashed back to Kimiko Taka. Something it had been doing too often in the past twenty-four hours.

Just because he'd told Kimiko what to wear didn't mean *he* was a stuffed shirt. He was the general manager, for God's sake. He was responsible for the image they presented. As a Taka, she ought to appreciate that fact. It was *his* problem he couldn't get the girl out of his head.

He focused on his mother. "In other words, you've already *quit* your job."

"No matter," she said swiftly. "I'll find another. You know that."

That was true enough. Mona Sherman had never had difficulty *finding* jobs. She could charm employment out of anyone. It was keeping them that had always been her challenge. He knew he could spend an hour arguing with his mother about the wisdom of her actions, or he could save himself the breath, since his arguments had never had any impact in the past. It was just always his job to clean up the mess afterward.

"What's Ralph's full name?" He wrote it on the pad next to his phone. "Does he have an address?" He was somewhat surprised when she provided one. He'd half expected her to blithely impart that Ralph had already moved in with her since the grapefruit rescue. "Take your cell phone in case something happens. I'll call the company and make certain you're covered for international calls."

"Don't be such a worrywart, Greggie. Now, I love you. Be sure you're taking those herbs I sent you. They'll keep your sex drive healthy."

He rolled his eyes. He lectured his living-in-the-sixties mother on taking her blood pressure medication.

She worried about him being able to get it up.

"Call and check in," he reminded, ignoring the herbal advice, much as he'd ignored the package. It might have made it through customs, but the box had been relegated, unopened, to the bottom of Greg's closet.

"I'll try," she said before hanging up. Which, in Mona-speak, meant *don't count on it*.

A soft sound behind him had him looking around.

Kimiko Taka stood in the open doorway of his office.

Yesterday she'd been the picture of brassy American boldness. Today she was the epitome of professionalism. Couture professionalism, anyway, he allowed, giving the cut of her closely tailored ice-blue suit an experienced eye. The just-from-bed tousled ringlets had been replaced by a sleek knot behind her head. Even her makeup was subdued. Her full bow-shaped lips looked soft and pink and unadorned, but that just made her wide, almond-shaped eyes stand out even more.

Unfortunately, she was no less attractive today than she had been yesterday. If his mother could see into his head, she'd realize that he needed no help from some damn herbs.

As for what Kimiko Taka was doing standing in his doorway? He had a sinking feeling in his gut. "Don't tell me HR sent *you*."

She looked genuinely puzzled. "Um, okay. I will not tell you." She lifted a folder at her side. "Grace asked me to come and have you sign off on these orders."

He let out a breath. God. He was losing it. Of course HR wouldn't have assigned Kimiko Taka to be his temporary assistant when he'd already told them to put her in sales. He waved her forward and took the folder from her to scrawl his signature where she indicated, then eyed her from across his cluttered desk. She wore a small hand-printed name badge on her lapel—a far cry from the engraved ones the rest of the staff already possessed. "You've obviously had your personnel orientation."

"This morning." She took the folder back from him. "It was very informative."

He glanced at his watch. "You've already toured the hotel?"

"Well, no. We did not get that done yet. I will return there during my lunch break for the tour. Grace was anxious for me to start. Evidently two people in her department called in this morning with the flu."

That made three staff members to bite the bug. Great. "You needn't give up your lunch break for a tour." Though he gave her points for being willing to do so. That is, if she'd actually follow through. Despite her impassioned speech after the staff meeting the evening before, he still questioned her commitment.

What did the girl want to work for, anyway? She was an heiress, for Christ's sake. She should be a *guest* in hotels like this, not some junior underling.

"I do not have any other plans for my lunch break," she said reasonably.

"How about eating?"

She looked at the tray sitting on one side of his desk that held the Western-style scrambled eggs and bacon that he'd never really gotten to. "Like you are doing?" She lifted the folder a little. "Thank you for the signatures." She turned as if to go, but paused. "I hesitate to tell you this, but—"

He was a fair-minded manager, he reminded himself. Or he was supposed to be despite his desire for some space from the disturbing young woman. "What is it, Ms. Taka?"

She moistened her lips. "Your shirt is misbuttoned." She smiled faintly and hurried out of his office. The hem of her skirt swayed slightly above her knees. Perfectly circumspect. Perfectly…perfect.

He forced himself to look away from the view she presented and looked down at his shirt and tie that he'd managed to forget all about.

She was right.

With a sigh, he began reworking the buttons.

Too bad he couldn't seem to realign his unwanted reaction to her just as easily.

Kimi was still smiling when she made it back to the sales and catering department. Aside from the office that Grace used, there were two others; one set up as a consultation room, and the other—far more spacious—housed several desks in an open area. It was to one of these desks that Grace had assigned Kimi. It had started out as empty as Mother Hubbard's cupboards, but, after just an hour, was now piled high with project files that Grace wanted her to quickly review so she was up to speed with the rest of the department members.

She left the folder on Grace's desk and headed to her own considerable pile of work. There were three other associates in the room, though, huddled over a round table spread with charts. They looked over at Kimi when she entered, barely returning her smiling hello, and she stifled a sigh, making herself approach them anyway. "Hi. I am Kimi Taka."

It was regrettably obvious that they already knew and had formed their opinions about her, too. It seemed that Greg's expectations about her fitting in with the rest of the staff members were all too accurate.

One of the group, a young dark-skinned woman who looked around Kimi's age, started to smile, but faltered at the fast looks she got from the others. But she still provided her name. "Tanya Wilson. Welcome to Kyoto," she added in a slightly southern-sounding rush.

Kimi's smile warmed a little in response. "Thank you." She looked at the other two—a natty blond guy in a beige suit who looked about her stepbrother Andrew's age, and a stylish woman who had probably been perfecting the art of looking down her nose in front of a mirror since she was five. Kimi stuck her hand out toward the snooty woman. "And you are…?" She lifted her eyebrows slightly.

The other woman did not quite have the nerve to ignore Kimi, though it looked like she wanted to. The handshake she gave, however, was limp. "Charity Smythe," she supplied with a bored clip. "And this is Nigel Winters." She spoke for the man, as if she did not trust him to speak for himself. "And as you can see, we're in the middle of a discussion."

Kimi wanted to swipe her hand down her skirt to wipe away the memory of that cold-fish handshake. Instead, she looked curiously at the charts on the table. Grace had already told her that the department worked as an ensemble regardless of who the lead person on a project might be. "Is this the Nguyen wedding?" She had been familiarizing herself with the details of the four-hundred-guest wedding to be held before Christmas when Grace had sent her to Greg's office.

Tanya nodded. "The problem is—"

"—there is no problem," Charity cut her off. "We're just finalizing some minor details." She swept up the floor charts and strode to the door. "Come along, Nigel. Tanya. *We* don't have time to sit around all morning twiddling our thumbs."

"Delightful meeting you," Nigel said quickly, as if sneaking it in before Charity could stop him. Then like two scurrying rabbits, he and Tanya sped after the departing woman.

As far as Kimi could tell, Charity seemed rather misnamed.

Kimi went to her desk and pulled the top file closer. An hour later, she had read through everything. If the quantity of special events on the department's plate were anything to go by, the Taka Kyoto was already proving to be a success.

Charity and crew had yet to return. She pushed away from the desk and started toward the coffee urn situated on a long counter that ran the back length of the room when Grace called her name. Kimi changed course and walked over to Grace's door. "Yes?"

"I suppose your coat is up in your room?" She barely waited for Kimi's surprised nod. "Run up and get it and meet me in the lobby. A car will take us to Osaka. I'd like you to sit in on a tour operator's meeting with me. Bring the mayoral luncheon and the Nguyen wedding files along. We'll review them on the drive."

Pleased, Kimi quickly sifted through the files on her desk, found the appropriate ones and took the service elevator up to her floor though it was less conveniently located than the lobby elevators were. The twenty-first floor was as still and silent as it had been since she had arrived, though a slender, elegantly decorated Christmas tree had appeared just across from the elevator bank. She had not verified it, but she was certain that she *was* the only one on the floor. By placing her in a completely different location than any other staff members who lived on site, Mr. Misbuttoned Sherman was following true to form by pointing out that she really was not one of them.

And unfortunately, that particular sentiment was evidently more widely shared than Kimi had anticipated.

Within minutes, she had retrieved her coat, exchanged the project folders for her laptop inside her briefcase and was heading back down again. She hurried back to the lobby only to slow her pace decorously when she spotted Grace in conversation with Greg.

Not that she had expected otherwise, but his starched white shirt now looked very correctly buttoned beneath the dove-gray tie he wore. She kept her gaze lowered deferentially as she stopped beside Grace; no one else need know that in doing so, her gaze was free to roam the undeniably perfect fit of Greg's dark gray trousers. The only thing marring the lines was the hand he had shoved in one pocket.

Or perhaps *mar* was the wrong term.

She moistened her lips and looked away from the way the fine wool tightened across his hips.

"Mark my words, Greg," Grace was saying. "The president

of Kobayashi Media will find some reason to blow off the mayoral luncheon. Oh, there'll be plenty of perfectly offered apologies and excuses, but I'll bet you a week's salary that he's a no-show."

"Excuse me." Kimi interrupted the breath that Grace had stopped to draw. "Shall I see if the driver is ready?"

"Thank you, dear." Grace did not look twice at Kimi.

The speculative glance that Greg gave her as she moved away, however, stuck in her mind throughout the drive to nearby Osaka, through Grace's meeting and through the return trip back again.

By the time their driver left them at the hotel once more, Kimi still was not certain why Grace had wanted to include her in the tour operator's meeting. But at the very least, it had been an interesting way to spend the morning, and it had been well away from the disturbing Mr. Sherman.

"I never realized how resorts and hotels vied for that sort of business," she admitted to Grace as they returned to their offices.

"We're all in it for a buck. Or, a yen—" Grace smiled "—as the case may be. Tourism is alive and well, even among—or particularly among—the high-end consumer that we court. The president of the local tour association is full of complaints that the Taka Kyoto is too cosmopolitan. Of course, he's related by marriage to a local official who bitterly opposed the building of the Taka in the first place. Your presence there this morning was a not-so subtle reminder to them that while the Taka *is* cosmopolitan *and* international, its roots are nonetheless of Japan. Taka is an important name in this country, and not just because of the TAKA-Hanson corporation." Grace patted Kimi's shoulder and pulled open the door to the stairwell. "Don't look so disappointed, dear."

"I am not disappointed," Kimi lied.

But Grace wasn't fooled. "Of course you are." Her voice echoed along with their footsteps. "You'd probably like everyone to forget who you are. To accept you purely based on your strengths and abilities."

"Is it that obvious?"

Grace smiled slightly. "Maybe not obvious, but perfectly understandable. Everyone wants to be loved unconditionally."

Kimi had never felt unloved by anyone who mattered to her. "Well-earned respect is what interests me," she admitted.

They had reached the lower level. Kimi couldn't help but look toward Greg's office, but the door was closed.

"The fact that you realize respect has to be earned is to your credit," Grace was saying, oblivious to Kimi's furtive glances down the hall. "Whether I told you my reasons for wanting you with me or not, you represented the Taka name admirably this morning."

Kimi skipped a little to catch up to her supervisor. "But I barely said a word."

"You didn't have to, my dear. They were all watching every move you did or did not make. How you greeted the other attendees, whether you were appropriately modest and deferential, whether you held to their highest ideals of good manners. And you did. You are a Japanese woman bearing a venerable name. They can find in you a suitable 'face' for the hotel, something that, for some, has been lacking."

"My father would be surprised to hear that. He finds me distressingly Americanized." She trailed after Grace into her office.

Grace's smile widened. "Then perhaps you combine the best of both worlds. The drive was useful, as well. I'm confident that you know the details of these two events inside and out. And since Charity's Japanese is still considerably less than perfect, I'm going to make you the point person for the Nguyen wedding." Her gaze skipped past Kimi's suddenly slack jaw. "Oh, good. Greg. I was hoping to catch you."

Kimi barely kept herself from whirling around.

"What's this about the Nguyen wedding?" he asked.

"I'm making Kimi the point person."

Kimi wanted to cringe. Even after just those few minutes with Charity, she could well imagine the other woman's reaction at being replaced at all, much less by Kimi. "Grace, I appreciate the confidence, but I have never—"

"Stop." Grace waved her hand. "We'll discuss it later. Just trust me when I warn you that, like Charity, you'll spend most of your time answering a dozen inane phone calls from their wedding coordinator. A truly impossible man named Anton. He's not French, however. He's wholly American, and from all accounts, excruciatingly tiresome. Now go on. I need to bend Greg's ear for a moment."

Kimi half-expected Greg to voice his protest that she would be given *any* level of responsibility—even one merely to field a fussy wedding coordinator's calls. But he didn't, and she headed back to her desk. Tanya was on the telephone and looked to be taking copious notes, and Nigel was at the wide whiteboard that hung on one wall, writing entries in the calendar-style grid.

Kimi had no messages waiting for her, and she scrawled a note that she was taking a lunch break and placed it in front of Tanya, who glanced at it before giving an absent wave.

Kimi didn't need lunch, however. She needed to finish her employee orientation. Namely, she needed to tour the entire facility. And now that she was point person on an actual event, it seemed even more important.

She took the wedding file with her, just in case she needed to make notes for herself, and went back to Human Resources. Unfortunately, the girl who was supposed to conduct the tour had gone home sick. Instead, Kimi was handed a detailed map with instructions to visit all the highlighted areas and sent on her solitary way.

With no better idea where to begin, Kimi decided to start from the ground floor and go up. Or, as the case was, two floors below ground level, where the soaring exhibition space sat hollow and silent except for the muted sound of power tools coming from somewhere nearby. She skipped the office floor since she had already seen most of it, as well as the main lobby level, and went up to the third floor where the first of the ball-rooms were. There were two here, with a combined reception capacity of nearly six hundred. It was pleasing to see that the interiors looked fully completed.

She was standing beneath the enormous crystal chandeliers that hung from the grand ballroom's ceiling when she felt the back of her neck prickle.

It was enough warning that she managed not to startle when Greg spoke. "They're stunning. Ally Rogers had the chandeliers specially designed for the space. She was here last week overseeing their installation."

Kimi's grip tightened on the project folder, afraid he just might yank it out of her grasp. "All of the interiors that have been completed are stunning," she agreed. She had never personally met Ally Rogers, but knew that the interior designer had stepped in to finish the San Francisco site when there had been problems with the original designer. She caught the tip of her tongue between her teeth for half a second but still could not refrain from asking. "Are you following me?"

He gave her a sideways glance. "Is that what it seems like?"

"Do you ever answer a question directly?"

"I'm in Kyoto now." The corners of his mouth kicked up ever so slightly, but it was still enough to make Kimi's breath catch. "Where all direct answers are often distinctly…indirect. But to answer your question, yes. I am following you. I heard you were here on your own."

Kimi waved the folded map. "Even I can follow a floor plan."

He let her acerbic tone pass. "Your…Mrs. Taka-Hanson called me while you were out with Grace."

"Checking up on me?" She might have expected that from her father but not necessarily Helen.

"She does have business with me here that doesn't concern you." His voice was mild, but Kimi still felt a flush burn through her skin.

She refrained, however, from asking why he had bothered to even tell Kimi about the call at all.

"I assured her that we were all doing our best to assimilate you into the fold as quickly as possible." His voice was inscrutably smooth.

"I am sure she was greatly comforted."

"Are *you* always sarcastic?"

She lowered her chin slightly. "My most humble apologies if you have found this to be true."

"I think I prefer the Kimiko Taka who stares me in the face when she has something to say."

She peered up at him through her lashes.

He made a muffled sound she could not interpret, and then he did slide the thick project file right out from her grasp.

Her lips parted, dismayed. "Please do not take it away from me, Greg—Mr. Sherman. I know the wedding budget is substantial and that I have no real experience with—"

He lifted his hand. "It is up to Grace to distribute her projects. I trust she knows what she's doing." Even though he did not sound entirely confident of it. "I was merely intending to carry it for you."

"Oh." Her lips slowly closed but suspicion quickly reared. "Like you would do for a guest?"

His lips twisted slightly. "I'd like to think it's just habit to carry a lady's books." He nodded at the map. "What else is on the agenda?"

Bemused, she looked from him to the glossy page. "Um, the rest of the meeting rooms, I guess."

"Let's go, then. You can lead the way since you're such an experienced floor-plan reader."

"You're coming with me?"

"Don't look so appalled, Taka-san. I *do* know the facility, and I might take it personally." He extended his arm, waiting for her to precede him from the elegant ballroom.

She quickly walked ahead of him, working hard to school her thoughts before the man realized that it was not horror that had her senses leaping all over themselves.

If anything, it was the opposite.

Chapter Four

"Ante up, old man," Shin told Greg as they sat around a small table in Seven, the otherwise empty lounge located on the seventh floor. It was Friday night; it was late, and as had become their habit over serving together off and on at various establishments for the past ten years, Shin, Grace, Greg and Lyle Donahue—their I.T. guru—were in for cards.

"Who's old?" Greg tossed in his coins. They played for money, but only enough to make things interesting and never enough to cause problems. After several hands already, the pot was pretty evenly divided between Shin and Greg. "If I'm not mistaken, Shin, you're the old man here." He studied his cards. Garbage. "So what was this about you firing a security guard this afternoon?"

"He was drunk and, while following up for the report, I learned he'd also been coming on to our newest and most celebrated staff member."

Greg stilled. "And you didn't tell me this earlier because... why?"

Shin glanced at him. "Because Danny Nelson's dismissal was from inebriation while on duty, not because his taste in women is pretty excellent." His lips quirked. "From what Kimi told me, she handled herself more than capably. You can read the report yourself. Might prove to be entertaining bedtime reading."

Thoughts about Kimiko Taka were already disturbing Greg's nighttime, and she'd only been there three days. He didn't need to exacerbate the problem. "You should have told me."

Shin arched an eyebrow. "It was a pretty standard situation, Greg."

"Not when it involves our owner's daughter."

"What do you think she's going to do?" Grace asked humorously. "Complain to them that a young man was flirting with her? Either you really have been focusing on just business for too long, or you've gone blind. Every heterosexual male who comes within ten feet of her is naturally drawn to flirting with her. She's an engaging, beautiful young woman. I think even Nigel was flirting with her this morning, and *he* openly prefers men. Frankly, I was heartened to see it—not the flirting because I really couldn't care less about that—but the fact that he was being friendly at all to Kimi considering how pissed off Charity is that she lost the Nguyen event to her. It's high time Nigel starts thinking for himself or he'll never go anywhere with Charity keeping him down. If she weren't an asset in so many other ways, I'd be wondering if I'd done the right thing agreeing to bring them here from Tokyo."

Greg rubbed his thumb along the edge of his cards. A pain was settling in behind his forehead. What other things was he in the dark about? "You didn't tell me there was dissension in your ranks."

"I also didn't call a special meeting to tell you that we're getting the Christmas trees placed and decorated on each floor or that our electric stapler is on the fritz." Grace was eyeing him closely. "Everything is still business as usual, Greg. Shin's exactly right. This is all just standard stuff, so what's *really* bothering you?"

He ignored the question, though he knew Grace was right. He didn't practice micromanaging. He expected his department heads to handle their department matters. So what made it different now?

Kimiko Taka, that's what.

Focusing his thoughts took more effort than he liked. "How many security officers do we still need, Shin?"

"After today, eight. We might have to transfer over a few from San Fran. Even temporarily, if that's what it takes. Just to get us through the New Year. As for the grand opening gala, we're running clearance now on the temps we'll add on for that night."

"I'll call the GM in San Francisco and see if anyone's willing to transfer. Can you at least fill the schedule for the mayor's luncheon without needing to pull on temps?" It wasn't the cost that was an issue; it was ensuring the temporary security officers had the proper security background checks.

Shin nodded. "Unless Grace has added even more attendees." He looked across at her.

"Not since this morning," she assured. "We've lost an attendee, too." She shot Greg an I-told-you-so look. "Yoshi Kobayashi sent his regrets this morning, though his office most humbly assures us the next in command at Kobayashi Media will be very honored to attend."

"What does it matter?" Their fourth, Lyle, was rarely concerned with anything that didn't involve a computer and his almighty cyberspace.

"It's an insult to the mayor, Lyle." Grace shook her head as if it were obvious. "They're going to use our first event as a forum for their dignified pissing contest over their opinions about the Taka even being built. I fold." She dropped her cards onto the table and wandered to the window that overlooked the city. "There's no place quite like Japan. Astonishing beauty. Amazing hospitality. Magnificently subtle barbs. How's Bridget?"

"Still out. We need to ensure that all the staff has an opportunity to get their flu shots, if they haven't already. Better late than never. Eight percent of our crew called in sick today." Greg squared his cards and raised the bet. Lyle never could bluff worth peanuts. Greg wasn't quite so sure about Shin's hand yet.

"Well, I'll take my chances with my vitamins because nobody is coming near me with a needle." Grace was emphatic. "Anyway, I'm tapped out, so I'm going to leave you little boys to your games and go home to reacquaint myself with my husband. Play nice, now." She headed out of the room.

But instead of settling back into the game once Grace departed, it soon broke up. Shin ended up the big winner. "It'll buy me a Starbucks in the morning," he said wryly, pocketing the change. With Lyle and Shin's departure, Greg slowly shut down the lights in the lounge and left, too.

Going down to his room on the fourth floor didn't appeal. Despite the hour, he was too restless. He tried his office, but even the matters awaiting him there didn't succeed in holding his attention for more than a few hours.

When he realized he'd reread the same paragraph of a memo from Housekeeping for the third time, he scrubbed his hands down his face and shoved away from the desk. He took the stairs up to the ghostly lobby level.

The perimeter lights were still lit, casting a golden wash down the unfinished walls. His shoes squeaked slightly on the concrete floor as he headed up the curving staircase, looking down at the nearly completed reception area. From his vantage point on the curving stairs, he could see the dark-eyed gleam of the blank built-in computer monitors behind the high desk. In just a few weeks, those monitors would be constantly alive, 24/7. For now, they looked like mysterious black holes.

He continued up to the mezzanine and paced past the glass-fronted shops—he'd just inked the deal to fill the last space with a New York shoe designer—and at the end of the looping floor, found himself at the elevator.

He *should* go to his room. Get a decent night's sleep for once.

Instead, he let out a long breath and pushed the button for the twenty-first floor. The soft strains of a koto and shakuhachi flute masked the faint hiss of the elevator. He ordinarily found the music soothing. Now, the meditative tones only underscored his disquiet.

He watched the clock-hand floor indicator smoothly tick its way around the half circle. Another moment and the doors slid open and he stepped off. His hand held the elevator door open, and he eyed the closed door of the suite at the end of the long hall.

What the hell was he doing? It was nearly midnight.

Exhaling a soft oath, he removed his hand, and the elevator door silently closed.

He walked to the end of the hall and rapped on the thick mahogany door. There was no response, and he knocked harder. Still no response.

He scrubbed his hands down his face. Was it lack of sleep muddling his head, or was it just *her?*

Midnight or not, it was Friday night. She was Kimiko Taka, the spoiled heiress whose nightlife and social exploits had been well-documented since she'd been a teen. Of course she was out sampling the night life, not the least bit affected by her encounter with the drunken security officer.

Calling himself ten kinds of a fool, Greg turned on his heel and strode back to the elevator. The doors slid open immediately and he jabbed the button for the next floor up. The top floor, which was occupied only by their fine-dining restaurant, Sakura, and an outdoor, roof-top garden.

He let himself out into the garden area, welcoming the slam of cold air that met him. The sky was clear, the stars overhead overwhelmingly bright, as if he could reach up and touch them. With far too little appreciation for the garden—designed by an award-winning landscape architect—he walked to the protective stone wall that kept curious visitors from venturing too close to the edge of the building and braced his hands on top of it, staring out.

His world was hotels, and this hotel was his. At least as much his as was possible.

So why couldn't he feel at home yet in his world?

He exhaled roughly and turned his back on the view. If he were more honest with himself, he'd be wondering if he would *ever* feel at home in this world.

He was a California hippie's brat who'd scraped his way up the ladder of the hospitality industry filling any and every job that came his way. From Housekeeping to Engineering to Catering to Front Office. If it had involved a paycheck and getting him closer to never having to worry if he and his mother would have a roof over their heads that night or not, he'd done it.

He'd been managing a small midlevel chain hotel by the time he was twenty-three, working on his graduate degree in night classes at the same time. He'd moved up and away from California, and up again.

Always better properties.

Always more money.

Now Greg had made it to the very pinnacle. He knew what he was doing and what he was capable of doing. But that didn't mean that he really belonged there.

He was still the same hungry kid from California whose mom had more often than not been high on the marijuana she'd bought with his lunch money.

The idea that he'd own his own hotel had been just an outlandish fantasy. Until he'd worked his way to this moment. This place.

He could conquer the Taka.

Would he be able to conquer what came after?

More annoyed with his thoughts than ever, he went back inside.

Through the dim gloom of the darkened restaurant, he could see a soft light burning from the open-styled kitchen and headed toward it. "Lorenzo? You've already redesigned your menu five times, and we haven't even opened the doors up here, yet." He stuck his head over the long glass-topped sushi bar to look toward the source of the light.

The wide eyes staring back at him from the light of a double-wide commercial refrigerator most definitely did not belong to Greg's six-foot-tall temperamental Italian head chef.

"Kimi." Her name escaped him.

She seemed to unfreeze then and nervously moistened her lips as her hip nudged the door closed. The soft light gleaming up from the base of the sushi bar was the only thing that kept them from total darkness. "I am sorry. I probably should not be in here." Her voice was low.

For some reason, his was, too. "If Lorenzo finds out you've been rooting around in his territory, he'll have a fit." The kind he'd thrown each of the times he'd discovered Greg foraging in one of the hotel's kitchens for a quick bite in the middle of the night.

"Add him to the list," she murmured.

"List?"

She shook her head slightly, and the hair that was pulled back in a tousled ponytail gleamed darkly. "Never mind."

"Why *are* you up here?" The question seemed obvious, given the collection of fresh vegetables clutched against her breast. But it was such a different setting than what his mind had conjured that he was still absorbing the surprise. "There are kitchens here that are actually open, you know."

"This seemed quicker. I just needed a bite before…" She shrugged again and moved over to the prep table, flipped on the task light, then dropped the vegetables on top and selected a knife.

"*Before*…what?"

She slid a look over her shoulder at him, then turned back to her vegetables. With a whack she severed a carrot in half. "Before bed."

The answer was ready and smooth, and for some reason he didn't buy it.

He rounded the sushi bar and walked back to where she was deftly chopping the carrots into bite-sized sticks. He snuck one and popped it into his mouth, crunching down on it.

"That is my supper you are eating," she pointed out.

"If you subsist on carrots and cucumbers, it's no wonder you're so tiny." He stole a slice of cucumber when it fell off her flashing knife.

"Yes, well, if I ever need a supply of herbs for stamina, I will know who to come to."

He slowly swallowed the crisp slice, his face flushed. "So you did overhear that particular bit from my mother."

Her gaze flew up, her lips parting. "That was your *mother?*"

"I do have one."

Her lips compressed. "Obviously. I cannot imagine many mothers broach that sort of subject with their sons, though."

"She's…unique," he allowed. "I'm surprised you managed to refrain from commenting this long."

"I will not mistake that as flattery." She swept the vegetables into a small bowl. "But I will be sure to pass on to Helen that your diligence has you prowling the darkened corners of your hotel even this late at night. I am certain she will be most impressed."

"And she'll be interested, no doubt, when I report on your nighttime feeding habits. Are you a vegetarian or something?"

"No. I just like vegetables. And maybe you and I should agree to refrain from reports of any kind."

A fine idea if he really believed that she wouldn't run to Mama and Papa under the right provocation.

He eyed her ivory face, searching for signs of what, he didn't know. "What happened with the security guard today, Ms. Taka?"

"A minute ago, it was Kimi." She flipped the end of her ponytail over her shoulder and took the knife to the sink. For a moment her shoulders seemed to bow beneath the brilliant pink T-shirt she wore.

He was so surprised by the vulnerability that seemed to suddenly sigh out of her that his hand started to lift toward her.

"I should have known Mr. Endo would end up telling you about it." She rinsed the knife and turned back to replace it, and her smooth smile seemed determinedly back in place. "But as I assured him, it was absolutely nothing."

He fisted his hand and lowered it to his side. "I'll be the judge of that. Tell me what happened. Exactly." He wanted to hear it from her lips, not from the printed report that Shin had filed.

"Very well, *Mr.* Sherman." She swiped a towel over the chopping block then tossed it onto the stainless steel table. "At exactly three twenty-seven, Security Officer Nelson and I were in the service elevator where he thought to impress me with his amazing wit, and once we left the elevator, he thought to impress me with his less than amazing dexterity." She picked up her bowl and went to slip past Greg, but he caught her arm.

She stopped, not looking at him. He hadn't been exaggerating that she was tiny, but right then it seemed to strike him all over again.

Everything about her seemed feminine. Delicate.

And in his head he formed an image of Danny Nelson. Not as tall as Greg, but easily as heavy.

He willed his fists to uncurl. "Kimiko." His voice was low. Warning.

"I prefer Kimi."

"I prefer a straightforward answer."

She exhaled. "It was nothing," she insisted. "He merely told an off-color joke that he probably never would have if not for the sake on his breath, and tried to grab my...my hind quarters. Okay?"

"No, it's not okay!" He pulled her around slightly, until he could see her face. "Shin said the guy came on to you. He didn't say he tried to assault you."

"There was no reason to tell Mr. Endo, when it was more than apparent that Nelson's tail was already in a sling for working under the influence. I have dealt with worse than an attempted pinch on the rear, I assure you." She wriggled her arm.

The motion had the soft side of her breast nudging his knuckles, and he quickly released her. "I suppose you have had plenty of practice, considering all those romantic exploits you've packed into your short life that we get to read about in the gossip rags."

She tossed back her head. "I am surprised you even admit to looking at such things."

"This isn't the only first-class hotel I've run," he drawled. It was only the most important one. "Do you think I haven't dealt with my share of celebrities and the media coverage they get?"

"I am not a celebrity."

"No, you're just the beautiful heiress who sleeps with them."

She looked pained. "I never—oh, for pity's sake. I dated *one* celebrity, and that was only because we happened to meet on campus at my university where he was giving a speech at a fund-raising dinner."

"You went to the Oscars with him. You sunbathed topless with him in Monte Carlo."

"I was not topless, and what does it matter, anyway?"

"He's old enough to be your father."

She laughed. "Right. If he had been a very precocious eleven-year-old. Have you been following my exploits for long, Mr. Sherman, or just reading up on them since you found yourself saddled with me?" Her eyes were unreadable as she leaned closer. Her long ponytail slid silkily over her shoulder and her voice sank even more. Goading. "Tell me. Did you like what you saw in those photographs?"

He'd never seen them. Only heard about them, like half of the rest of the world. And her softly accented whisper was *not* getting under his skin. "I couldn't care less about celebrity gossip," he assured smoothly. "I care about what happens under the roof of this hotel. Which brings me right back to you, and Danny Nelson's assault."

She straightened again and swept back her hair. "Wandering hands," she corrected briskly. "Most men I have met seem to be afflicted with the condition at one point or another."

"Maybe because you dress to invite it."

"Blame the victim, is that it? I assure you, Mr. Sherman, I was dressed most circumspectly today, per your decree. So, tell me, just how my wearing a tweed suit could possibly inflame Mr. Nelson?"

"Honey, you could wear burlap and drive a man right around the bend, and you damn well know it."

"Oh, the compliments." She pressed the back of her hand to her forehead. "They are overwhelming me."

What the hell had happened to this conversation? He ought to know better than to enter verbal skirmishes with rich little girls. Or to enter into anything, for that matter. "I expect everyone who enters the Taka to be safe. Whether they're guests or…employees."

"Ooh." She pursed her lips. "That is such a hard word for you to say when it comes to me."

Unfortunately, words weren't the only things that were hard when it came to her. "You don't exactly fit the job description. *Any* of them."

"Only because you want to think that way."

He snorted. "Typical employees usually don't occupy one of the best suites in the house," he reminded.

"You are the one who put me there."

"Do you think I had a choice?" He grabbed another carrot stick out of her bowl, avoiding the hand she slapped at him.

"Playing at your job here is one thing. Sticking you in a standard room on the fourth floor with no view and few frills is hardly what the boss's daughter is accustomed to."

"Maybe you're just afraid to have me on the fourth floor with you." She leaned closer again. Close enough that the silky end of her ponytail drifted over his forearm as tickling and as taunting as the faint smile that played around her soft, perfectly sculpted lips. Her voice dropped again in that nearly intimate whisper. "That *is* where your room is, is it not, Greg?"

He deliberately brushed her ponytail away from his arm. "Rein it in, Kimi. I'm not interested."

"Are you certain?"

"I don't play with precocious children." The last time he'd tried, he'd been twenty-five and Sydney just twenty-two. She hadn't been an employee or the daughter of his boss. But she had been a guest of the hotel where he'd worked, and he'd still ended up chewed thoroughly and spat out when she'd decided his pedigree wasn't up to snuff.

She tilted her head, looking at him from the corner of her exotic eyes. "Or you are afraid to play with the daughter of your boss."

"Look at it however you like, Ms. Taka. No matter how you turn it—employee, boss's daughter, whatever. You're forbidden fruit."

"Is that not the sweetest kind?" She took the carrot from his fingers that he'd forgotten all about and slipped it between her lips. As if by magic, her knowing, taunting expression disappeared, leaving only a very young woman sneaking out for an oddly lonely nighttime vegetable raid. "Now, if we are through with this odd little inquisition, I have homework. Some work I have brought home, I mean. So bill the food to my suite."

"There *is* no bill for your suite," he reminded. "Seeing as your parents own it."

"Then please convey my thanks to Chef Lorenzo."

"And invite him to have both our heads? Don't think so. I'd rather him think there are rabbits sneaking into his fridge."

"Then I guess I will go." She cradled her small bowl of vegetables and ducked past him, quickly weaving around the guest tables toward the door.

"Ms. Taka."

Reluctance screamed from her when she stopped again and looked over her shoulder. "Yes?"

"You're sure you are all right?"

Even in the thin light from the kitchen behind them, he could see the softening in her expression. "Yes. Quite sure."

"Okay. Enjoy your weekend." Unless there was some special need, Grace's department enjoyed a Monday-through-Friday work week.

She pressed her lips together for a moment, her eyes wider than ever. "Thank you. You, too." Then, almost shyly—which still seemed difficult to fathom given the direction their conversation had taken—she disappeared through the arching entry that led back to the elevator.

A moment later he heard the low elevator chime and then all was silent and still.

Greg realized he was rubbing his knuckles against his shirt.

Danny Nelson supposedly had the excuse of too much sake.

What excuse did *he* have?

He yanked open the refrigerator, found a fresh carrot for himself and picked up the house phone next to the walk-in freezer. Even though the hotel was not yet hosting guests, Shin's department was operating around the clock with at least a skeleton crew on duty to monitor the facility. "This is Sherman. I want the service elevators put on the closed-circuit system," he told the security officer who answered his call. "Use portable units for tonight if you have to, but get the work scheduled by morning."

"Yes, sir."

He hung up. There would be complaints from employees who would consider the measures to be intrusive, but at this point, he didn't care. Shin had wanted every elevator on the system in the first place.

Greg should have listened to him.

He snapped off the light and crunched off the end of the carrot, taking the service elevator straight down to his office.

Well beyond the temptation of Kimi and the Mahogany Suite.

In her suite, Kimi stared at her laptop and the accumulation of study materials spread across the desk. She had four hours left to finish her exam and get it submitted to her Principles of International Business professor. An incomplete for the course would mean no diploma at the end of the semester, and she was counting on adding that ammunition to her work here in Kyoto when she prevailed upon her parents to find a spot for her back in the States.

Unfortunately, the only thing her mind seemed willing to focus on was Greg.

He was a stiff-necked, humorless, by-the-book manager.

Except when he was not being stiff-necked or humorless, a tormenting voice inside her slyly whispered. Either way, he was the sexiest man she had ever met.

No amount of herbs could make him more lethal than he already was.

She jabbed a key on the keyboard, sending her swirling psychedelic screen saver into la-la land, peered at the examination form and tucked a carrot stick between her teeth.

But the second she did that, the memory of Greg snatching the piece while she had been chopping slid into her head.

All he had done was give a glimpse into his humanity, and her silly heart was reacting as if he had slain dragons for her.

It was no wonder women made fools of themselves all the time where men were concerned. She had just never before counted herself as one of them.

She wondered what he would have to say if he ever learned that her romantic exploits had generally ended at her door. She had fended off her share of passes, and certainly ones less easily avoided than the clumsy security guard's grope. What she had *not* done, however, was ever sleep with any of the men.

What a good laugh Greg would have if he knew that she was a virgin.

She pressed her forehead into her palms. But that was not even the worst of it.

He was the first man she had ever met who really made her yearn to change that particular fact.

With him.

Chapter Five

"Okay, children." Grace Ishida stood at the project board that Nigel had trimmed with silver garland, her hands on her hips. It was Tuesday, and she had called her department together for a brief meeting before lunch. "Crunch time. As we all well know, the mayoral luncheon is tomorrow. There'll be a great deal of local media present." Her lips twisted slightly. "It is imperative that we make a good showing. Unfortunately—" she looked around the room "—as we all *also* know, our banquet crew has been falling victim to this damn bug that's working its way through our system. Literally. We're short six servers, and I'm looking for volunteers."

A host of groans went around, but Grace looked undeterred. "Come on, now. Charity, you used to work banquets."

The woman shook her head, looking bored. "Fortunately I'm long past those menial days."

Grace's expression did not falter as she continued surveying the crowded room. "Anyone? We're pulling from all departments, but I would think at least *one* of you would be willing to pitch in."

Kimi looked around the room. Not a single person appeared interested in helping out. She chewed the inside of her lip for a moment, then tentatively raised her hand. "I'm willing."

Sitting just a few seats from her, Charity made a show of trying to muffle a snort.

Kimi's hand went up even more firmly. She met Grace's gaze. Her supervisor gave Kimi the courtesy of not showing her skepticism as noticeably as Charity had, but it was still there all the same.

Kimi lowered her hand. "I may not have *served* any banquets, but I have attended hundreds of them. I think I can manage to act the part, if nothing else."

Grace smiled faintly. "All right." Her gaze traveled over the rest of the assembly. "Hopefully there'll be others in this house who'll step forward. In the meantime, we'll move on to a couple of other points of business—"

"Grace?" Tanya Wilson sat closer to the edge of her seat. "I'll work the banquet, too."

"So will I." Another hand went up. Then another.

Charity's hand, noticeably, was still not one of them. But Grace was obviously pleased, nonetheless. "Well done," she said. "You'll need to report to the banquet kitchen tomorrow morning by eight, but it would be wise for you to go by sometime today and pick up a uniform."

She went on to quickly discuss the mini-clinic Greg had arranged that afternoon for staff members to receive flu shots and the scheduling of the staff's holiday party, then sent them all back to their duties. But she stopped by Kimi's desk as she headed toward her office. "Kimi? Could I have a word?"

"Of course." She rose, avoiding Charity who was looking entirely too superior, and followed Grace into the other woman's office.

Grace closed the door. "Sit down," she invited, waving at the two seats positioned in front of her untidy desk.

Unaccountably nervous, Kimi sat and Grace took her own seat behind her desk. She rested her arms on top, her hands clasped together and eyed Kimi. "Thank you for volunteering the way you did."

"I want to help," Kimi said, fully prepared for Grace to tell her that she did not want her inexperienced assistance. "I can pour ice water and set out butter curls just as well as the next person," she assured.

Grace's smile widened. "I'm sure you can. If you hadn't set the example, I doubt anyone else would have felt shamed into volunteering at all. No, I'm afraid I brought you in to ask another favor of you."

"Anything."

"Well, it's about Yoshi Kobayashi. He's president of Kobayashi Media, and it would be really good if we could get him to the luncheon. So far he's refused. I'm wondering if you'd be willing to lend your…encouragement…to him and see if he'll change his mind about attending."

"What can I do?"

Grace eyed her steadily. "Your father runs the TAKA-Hanson Corporation. There is no larger media enterprise in this part of the world. That alone would have weight with Kobayashi."

"Yes, my *father* runs TAKA," Kimi emphasized. "I'm only fortunate that they are letting me in the door with the new hospitality division."

"We certainly don't want to disturb your father or stepmother about this—" Grace shook her head, looking wryly aggravated "—this matter that is probably very minor in the grand scheme of things. I just want our first event to be as perfect as it can possibly be."

Kimi sighed faintly. How could she refuse? "I will see what I can do."

Grace smiled. "I knew I could count on you."

"Excuse me." Tanya popped her head into the office. "Kimi, Anton Tessier is here to see you."

"Thanks, Tanya." Kimi rose and looked at her supervisor. "If you will excuse me?"

Grace waved her along. "Of course."

A full hour later, Kimi had a fresh page of notes from the wedding coordinator about the big Nguyen wedding. She also had a not-so-fresh headache from wondering how she was supposed to solve Grace's problem with Kobayashi Media.

But at least she had things to keep her mind occupied, lest she fall back into the preoccupation with her general manager that had consumed most of her weekend.

After her encounter with Greg on Friday night, she had finally completed her exam and gotten it submitted barely before the deadline, then had spent the rest of the weekend almost entirely in her suite, either studying or sleeping and trying to conquer all wayward thoughts about the tall, green-eyed man. She had ventured out only once to use the swimming pool on the seventeenth floor when she had been certain nobody would be the wiser.

And yesterday, she had heard that he was in Tokyo for most of the day on business.

But her first glimpse of Greg as she walked with Anton through the lobby plainly pointed out that she had not managed to conquer a single thing, least of all her wayward thoughts or her unruly hormones.

For one thing, he did not have on his suit coat, which was a surprise in itself, since aside from that morning when she had gone to his office with Grace's papers, she had not seen him without one.

Pity, too, because the man truly had a world-class physique.

For another thing, he was standing eight feet up a ladder in the chaotic lobby, arms wide as he gestured and discussed the

Venetian plaster finish the workers perched on the scaffolding were installing.

Greg's Japanese was perfect. But his gesturing was definitely all American.

And she…she felt disconcertingly *all* female.

With no small amount of effort, she dragged her gaze from the muscles outlined beneath his finely tailored white shirt and continued accompanying the wedding coordinator through the obstacle course the lobby had become thanks to the combined confusion of new scaffolding and the marble tile that was being laid.

Grace had been accurate about the man's fussy nature. Considering how much his clients were spending on their wedding, though, Kimi figured they were purchasing the right to be particular even if some of their choices seemed thoroughly extravagant to her.

What was the point of having a twelve-layer wedding cake flown in from New York at an exorbitant cost when the hotel possessed a world-class pastry chef who could have easily created the same towering confection?

She must have been doing a decent job of hiding her personal feelings, though, because Anton seemed completely satisfied as he clasped her hand between both of his and bowed enthusiastically before finally heading down the wide, shallow steps that fronted the hotel.

Kimi turned around to go back to her office. She was not going to bother Helen or her father about Kobayashi. But she *could* call her stepsister, Jenny Warren, who had worked for TAKA-Hanson's media division before Helen had tasked her more recently with media relations for the new hospitality division.

But all of those thoughts siphoned out of her head when she nearly walked right into Greg.

He was off the ladder now, talking with the chief engineer who was holding what looked like copies of blueprints, and he caught her arm to steady her when she slipped on the concrete. "Are you all right, Ms. Taka?" His green gaze was impersonal.

"I'm fine. Pardon me." She smiled at the chief engineer and quickly veered around the still-dry fountain, putting Greg safely out of her line of sight. But when she ended up face-to-face with Charity Smythe and the animosity pouring from her, Kimi almost wished that she had taken her chances with Greg.

"I don't know who you're trying to impress," Charity said just loud enough for Kimi to hear. "But I guarantee that you're not going to be the favored darling of the management when you make a fool of yourself tomorrow."

"By management, you mean Mr. Sherman?" Kimi managed a blithe tone. If the other woman knew just how *un*favored Kimi was, she would probably turn cartwheels right there among the pallets of marble tile. "I am surprised that you did not volunteer to help at the banquet, yourself. At least then you could personally witness my humiliation."

"This isn't a joke, you know." Charity's voice went from cold to icy.

"I would never presume to think it is." Kimi stared the other woman in the face. "I *am* a Taka, Charity. Do you not think I might have a vested interest in the success of a venture that bears my name?"

"You're a Taka, and you'll never let anyone forget it, will you?" Charity's teeth were practically bared.

"No, Charity. No one will forget it, despite what I want."

"Ms. Smythe. Ms. Taka." Greg's deep voice had both of them springing apart. "Is everything all right?"

"Right as rain." In a blink, the woman's expression had cleared. "If you'll excuse me, *I* have work to do." She strode off as if the Emperor of Japan himself was waiting for her.

"Is she giving you problems?"

Kimi turned back to Greg only to find her nose mere inches from the nubby silk of his tie. Did he always smell so good?

"What?" She slid back a step, frantically grasping for some functioning brain cells. "Charity? She's just being Charity." She sucked in her lower lip and felt the infinitely slow tick of time as his gaze narrowed on her face.

"Are you sure that's all?"

"Well, she loathes and detests me," Kimi managed lightly. "Not unlike others in these parts."

"Nobody loathes and detests you," he countered brusquely.

"I do not exactly have a fan club."

"You should have stayed in the States if you wanted that."

"I do not want a fan club," she corrected, wishing that she had kept her foolish mouth shut. No matter what she said or did around Greg, it tended to be the wrong thing. "Would you excuse me?"

His gaze did not waver from her face, but he nodded. "Of course."

She quickly walked away through the chaotic lobby.

Instead of returning to her basement office, though, Kimi took the service elevator up to the twenty-first floor. She would call Jenny. Sound her out. But she would do it from the privacy of her suite where nobody would be likely to overhear.

Given the time difference between Kyoto and Chicago, it was evening for Jenny when she finally came on the line. Kimi had long ago become close to the daughter that Helen had borne and given up while still a teenager, but not even Jenny— whose adoptive parents were highly successful hoteliers in their own right—seemed able to understand Kimi's intense desire to be judged on her own merits rather than the family's.

When Kimi explained the situation about the luncheon, though, Jenny had only one suggestion since she had never personally had any dealings with Kobayashi. "Call your grandfather," she advised. "Despite the softening of his ways since Mori and Helen married, he's still about as old school as it gets when it comes to business there, and his roots are a lot deeper."

Kimi knew only too well how deep, having spent a good amount of time with him in her early years. Those roots went nearly to the center of the earth.

"So," Jenny asked curiously, "how is everything *else* there going? Have you set the hotel on its ear yet?"

"I am not trying to."

Jenny chuckled. "All things are normal, then. I was just looking at the calendar here. Time's racing toward the gala, isn't it? Things are probably really hopping there. Are you finding the working world more to your liking than the academic one?"

She very nearly confided in Jenny that she had managed to get herself reinstated to finish her classes online, but did not. Her stepsister would be just as surprised as the rest of the family when Kimi showed off that diploma. "It is pretty much more of the same."

"You mean you're blowing off your duties just to see if somebody dares to get mad about it?"

"No!"

Even across the distance, Kimi could hear Jenny's faint sigh. "Well, that's what you did in school, sweetheart."

That was something Kimi could not deny. "I mean that people either blame me for being a Taka or love me only for being a Taka."

"I hate to tell you, Kimi, but you *are* a Taka."

"So get used to it?"

"Figure out a way to accept it," Jenny advised. "Regardless of your heritage, you should live your life the way you want to live it; not as a reaction to what everyone else does."

"That sounds like something Helen would say."

"Well—" Jenny's voice was serious "—it finally seems to have worked for her. Now come on. Have you made some new friends? What's Greg Sherman like? Helen has really good things to say about him."

"He is fine."

"Just *fine?* If Helen is not singing his praises, then Mori is."

Kimi swallowed. "Actually, I do not see all that much of him. I am pretty busy working in the basement sales office. The hotel is spectacular, though. At least it *will* be when the rest of the interiors are completed. How is Richard and the baby?"

"Oh-ho. Changing the subject. All right, I'll let you off the hook only to talk about my husband and my son, who are both as wonderful and handsome as ever. We've gotten to see a lot of Jack and Samantha lately, since he and Richard have been working together as legal counsel for the hospitality division. And my friend Samara and Richard's brother Steven are getting married, so there have been all the arrangements to make for that. It's been busy, to say the least. And of course, the entire family will be in Kyoto for the gala. Everyone is anxious to see how you're doing there."

Anxious was probably too accurate of a word, Kimi knew. "I am looking forward to seeing everyone, too." And having the satisfaction of announcing that she had earned her college diploma without them having to harp on her to the very end.

Once she had hung up with Jenny, Kimi stared at the telephone for a long moment. Then she snatched up the receiver again and quickly dialed.

Her grandparents, as she had anticipated, were thoroughly delighted to hear from her. But also, as anticipated, her grandfather refused to discuss anything with her over the telephone. Particularly anything business related. If she wished to discuss something with him, then she would need to visit them in Nesutotaka. The small village north of Tokyo was where her father had been born, and as far as Kimi was concerned, it was pretty much stuck in the feudal era. "*O-jii-san*, I am at work. I cannot just take the rest of the day to go running up to Nesutotaka."

"*Hai*. When you do have time, granddaughter, then we will talk."

Kimi did not *have* time. "If I take the train up there this afternoon will you at least first confirm whether or not you even know the president of Kobayashi Media?"

"You would negotiate with your grandfather?"

Kimi could not help but laugh a little. "When I was a girl and visiting you, you used to bargain with me over watching your television."

"Ah. So you do remember the time when you lived here."

She rubbed her forehead, keeping her voice light. "How could I forget?"

"I will meet your train," Yukio said. "Your grandmother will be most pleased." Without fanfare, he disconnected the call.

Kimi hung up, too, with a sigh, then went to find something appropriate to wear to visit her extremely traditional grandparents. If she wanted a favor from her grandfather, she had better go in as prepared as she could possibly get.

Unfortunately, Kimi's wardrobe had not included a kimono since she had been a schoolgirl. If Greg had taken issue with the brevity of her skirts, her grandfather would have been apoplectic. She did not have anything that extended well below the knee, and he never had been particularly accepting of women wearing jeans.

Painfully aware of the ticking time, she finally pulled out a pair of skinny gray slacks, paired them with flat-heeled black boots and a long, tailored white blouse. She called down to Grace's office, but she was out, so Kimi had to settle for leaving a message with Nigel that she would be absent for the rest of the afternoon. Then she quickly shoved one of her textbooks in a satchel and headed out.

With any luck at all, she would be back before too late an hour, and she could still get yesterday's class assignments done and still manage a few hours of sleep before she had to assume the thoroughly unfamiliar role of banquet server.

* * *

At first, Greg thought he was seeing things. That thoughts of Kimiko Taka had overtaken his waking hours as thoroughly as they had his meager sleeping ones. More than half of the servers silently working among the scarlet damask-draped tables were slender, dark-haired young women.

He smiled absently in response to the chattering woman on his right—the wife of Kobayashi Media's president who had, much to Grace's relief, decided to honor them with his presence after all—and scanned the tables.

There. There she was.

Pouring water from a pitcher into a gray-haired guest's glass with one hand, and clearing away an empty dinner plate with her other.

"Your ballroom has made a beautiful presentation, *buchō*," the woman said. "Did you intend to replicate my husband's favorite color, or is this a happy coincidence?" She smoothed her hand along the damask.

Since arriving in Japan, Greg had become accustomed to being addressed simply as general manager rather than by his name, and he gave her a smile even though he was tracking Kimiko's movements as she went back and forth among the four tables she was tending and the serving carts waiting against the wall. "At the Taka, no detail is too small for attention."

"I am certain my husband has already taken note of that." The husband, Yoshi, was sitting on the dais, alongside the mayor and their other particularly honored guests. "He has mentioned to me that he is most pleased with the addition of the Taka Kyoto to our modest skyline."

"That is undeserving praise, indeed." Early on, Yoshi had been a vocal opponent to the high-rise structure. "I hope we will have reason to see you and your husband here at the Taka again."

"I am certain of it. My husband most enjoys fine cuisine,"

she returned, looking pleased. "We have heard rumors that your chefs have no compare."

"Mr. Sherman, Mrs. Ishida wishes to remind you of the time." A soft-spoken young woman stopped next to him.

Greg thanked her, and the girl moved off. He excused himself from those at his table and moved up to the podium at the center of the two long tables.

"Konichiwa." He spoke easily into the microphone. "Good afternoon. I am Greg Sherman, general manager, and it is my great pleasure and honor to welcome all of you to the Taka Kyoto." With no effort, he continued his brief speech and acknowledgments of their honored guests, but he was still glad to surrender the podium to the mayor and return to his table.

While the mayor launched into his remarks, Greg's gaze homed in on Kimi again.

At this distance, there was nothing to distinguish her from the other servers. She wore the same stiff white shirt tucked into narrow black pants; had the same wide black satin cummerbund circling her narrow waist. Even her hair, twisted into a low knot at the nape of her neck, was a mirror copy to the other female servers.

Yet it *was* her.

Greg knew it even before he caught her glance when she sneaked a quick look toward the head table where he sat during one of her trips back toward her tables from the cart. Despite the distance of three hundred people between them, he felt the impact.

If the sudden hesitation in her otherwise smooth movements was any indication, so did she.

Not until the final course had been served and there was a break in the speeches, however, could Greg break away from the table.

He went straight through to the kitchen, moving easily through the beehive of activity there, and finally found her in the service corridor, perched on an overturned five-gallon bucket.

"Ms. Taka. Would you mind telling me what you think you're doing?" He stopped in front of her.

Her gaze warily lifted to his, and she wriggled her stocking-covered toes. "Well, I think I am rubbing my feet."

He grimaced. "Clearly."

"Do not worry," she said evenly. "I am finished in there until we start tearing down."

"What were you *doing* in there in the first place?"

She pushed her foot back into her low-heeled shoe and stood. Without the usual high heels he was used to seeing her wear, she seemed even more petite. "Serving," she said with exaggerated patience. "Was that not apparent?"

"Why?"

"Well, because in my infinitely spoiled manner, I decided to take some poor banquet server's position just for the fun of it!"

He let out a gusty sigh. "If I believed that—"

"Then why do you ask?"

"Because I don't know *what* to think when it comes to you."

"Yes, you do. You think the worst." Her voice was arid. "It's what comes most naturally for you."

"Ms. Taka—"

"I volunteered," she admitted, clearly exasperated. "Grace said they needed help today, and I offered."

He eyed her, trying to find some measure of judgment where she was concerned. But the further along they went, the harder he was finding it. "You look tired," he said abruptly.

Her hackles visibly rose, proving that his measure had definitely missed the mark.

She bowed her head slightly. "*Sumimasen*. Pardon me." Sarcasm screamed from the polite words.

"Maybe you should curtail the late-night ventures out," he advised.

Her eyebrows shot up. "Excuse me? I only raided the kitchen one time!"

"I was talking about *last* night."

"What about last night?"

"It was well after midnight before you returned to your room."

She pulled her head back, giving him a long look. "And the reason you know that?" Her hands went to her narrow hips. "What are you doing? Keeping track of my hours? Would that be for your benefit, Mr. Sherman, or are you reporting back to my father? Surely you do not imagine he would be shocked, do you? I mean, considering my well-known wayward ways."

"Lose the sarcasm," he suggested evenly. "No one is keeping track of you. And unless you want the entire hotel privy to your business, you might want to lower your voice."

"A good portion of the people working in this hotel already think they are privy to my business," she countered tartly, "most notably you. So what difference does it make? I was judged and categorized before I walked in the door. And if I am not being monitored, how do you know just how late it was before I returned to my room? Or was that merely a lucky shot in the dark?"

"Security, Ms. Taka," he supplied. "As you should well know, the public areas are monitored."

"Obviously, Mr. Sherman. Which is my point." She folded her arms and threw back her head, managing to look down her nose at him despite her significant lack of height. "Do you receive reports of all comings and goings of the employees, or am I just—" her lips curved in a dulcet smile "—particularly special to you?"

Temper snapped from her dark eyes despite the sweet smile, and once again he wished that he'd kept his bloody mouth shut. "I was in the security office, and I saw you on camera myself. And the only thing you need worry about is keeping your, oh, call them extracurricular activities, from affecting your job performance."

"Please, let us not be coy, Mr. Sherman. You think I was out partying."

"Were you?"

"Jealous?"

"I don't care who you're sleeping with." A larger lie hadn't fallen from his lips in a long time. "Just remember that we do have a drug-free work environment here. Not even you will be allowed any infractions."

She looked incensed—and a little hurt. "My mother died of a drug overdose. *I* have never touched them."

He hadn't known the cause of her mother's death; only that it had occurred when Kimi was very young. "I'm sorry. Nevertheless, you'll consider exercising some of that good judgment when it comes to …whatever else you're doing in the middle of the night."

"Visiting my grandparents," she snapped. "I spent more than half my day yesterday on the train to and from Nesutotaka, all so that you and the mayor could rub elbows with Yoshi Kobayashi this afternoon!"

He grabbed her elbow, keeping her from stomping back into the kitchen in a huff. "Explain."

"I thought I just did." She jerked out of his hold.

"*You* are responsible for Kobayashi attending the luncheon?" Grace had neglected to share that little nugget when she'd told Greg the Kobayashis were back on the attendee list.

"My grandfather is responsible," Kimi corrected witheringly. "A phone call from him is all it took."

Greg knew Yukio Taka by reputation only. The man had run the TAKA Corporation until Kimi's father, Mori, had taken over the media juggernaut when Kimi would have still been a child. The elderly man was retired, but Greg knew the man still had considerable sway in the country. Evidently enough sway to nudge Yoshi Kobayashi into a more favorable position where the hotel was concerned. "And this phone call involved you traveling until well after midnight."

"It was difficult to leave quickly. Now, if I had known that there was a curfew to be observed, I am sure my grandparents would have understood my need to catch an earlier train. You know," she ran on unstoppably, "most people would have to be really creative to find some way to say a few train rides could adversely affect my job performance, but if anyone can, I bet it will be you. Then again, you think I am just playing at the job, anyway, so what does it matter if you think my job performance is inadequate?"

"I didn't say your work was inadequate. I was warning you— oh, for—" He bit off an oath. She knew she was doing a perfectly decent job. And she undoubtedly knew that *he* knew it.

Which, more than ever, made him look like an overbearing, unreasonable boss.

Something he'd never considered himself to be.

Before her.

The problem was that despite the thoroughly regulation banquet uniform she wore, he still couldn't see her as his employee.

Because she was the owner's daughter?

Or because with each passing hour, he found himself in danger of *forgetting* that she was the owner's daughter?

"There is nothing wrong with your—"

She leaned forward a little, her lips pursing softly. "—performance," she supplied. As quickly as her eyes had filled with snapping temper, they now were sparkling with triumphant humor. "It is not such a hard word to say, Mr. Sherman. You just put your lips together and—" She breathed out a puffing "puh."

Despite everything, a bark of laughter escaped. "You really are something else, Kimi."

Her lips parted, surprise blanking everything else from her expressive face. "You…you laughed."

"Your amazement is condemning. Did you think I was incapable?"

"Hai." She blinked, as if shaking herself awake. "Yes. I am

sorry. I...maybe I did. Which was very rude of me." She glanced around, looking oddly shy. "I appreciate the vote of confidence—however warily given. But I...I should see if the banquet captain needs me yet. Excuse me."

She pushed back through the swinging door to the kitchen before Greg could stop her.

She'd had no reason why she should have explained her activities the night before to him. He wasn't her keeper, and she hadn't been on duty. It definitely wasn't her problem that he was the one having trouble sleeping—which was why he'd been roaming around the hotel in the first place.

But explain she had, and he felt even more like a bastard.

He shoved his hand through his hair and rejoined the banquet guests, and even though he kept an eye out for Kimi, she didn't appear inside the ballroom again.

Chapter Six

Thanks to Kobayashi Media, by the next morning it was a widely publicized fact that the Taka Kyoto was a wildly successful addition to Kyoto's overall excellence. The mayor's luncheon hosted there was an unqualified success.

Greg, however, didn't feel all that successful. Not when he knew he'd found at least one employee whom he didn't seem able to treat with his usual impartiality. The truth of that gnawed at him through a morning of meetings and interviews held in the training room, and it was still gnawing at him when he finally broke away long enough to head down to his office.

Both service elevators were humming, so he took the stairs only to encounter a roadblock in the form of the group coming up from the opposite direction, with Grace in the lead. They were all holding coats and scarves.

"Heating go out?" He wasn't entirely joking, since they'd

had similar problems that were supposed to have been resolved by now.

"No." She tossed her jacket over her other arm. "We're off on an unexpected field trip. I found out this morning that the children's orchestra you talked me into scheduling for the gala is performing this afternoon at a school in the area. We're going for a preview."

"So you can pull in another group if you figure they're not up to Taka standards?"

"Maybe." She grinned. "My boss expects me to cover all contingencies."

"As well he should." Greg looked past her to the rest of the group; all of the half dozen were faces he easily recognized. But it was the dark-haired woman in the salmon-colored suit bringing up the rear who predictably dragged at his attention. Kimi was a part of Grace's group, clearly. But she was also very much apart from Grace's group. Even he could see that. He also could see that she was looking everywhere but at *him*.

What else did he deserve?

"I'll go with you," he said abruptly.

To her credit, Grace managed not to gape at him in surprise. "We'll be gone through lunch and most of the afternoon," she warned. "Don't you have meetings scheduled this afternoon?"

He did. "They'll keep."

Her gaze was full of questions, but they'd worked together long enough that he knew she'd keep them to herself. At least for a while. "Great. Then you can put our lunch on *your* expense report, since my boss is always telling me I'm going over on mine." With a smile, she sidled past him up the steps, and the rest followed her.

Greg fell into line behind Kimi. The others had already reached the lobby-level door but several steps above him, she leaned her head back over her shoulder. "There is no need for you to play watchdog, if that is your intention," she said under her breath.

"I have more than the usual vested interest. I'm the one who suggested the children's group for the gala. Personally, I think they're pretty remarkable, and they can use the exposure they'll get that night to get more bookings. More bookings means more funds. More funds mean more instruments and more students."

"Oh." Her mouth closed. Pink rode her cheeks. "And now you undoubtedly believe I am more self-involved than ever."

His thoughts where she was concerned were best kept unshared. He passed her on the steps and reached the lobby door, holding it open for her.

Without looking at him, she hurried past, leaving that faint, intoxicating scent of hers in her wake.

He warned himself to get a grip and went to make arrangements for his absence that afternoon.

Grace had already scheduled one of the hotel limos to transport her group. His presence didn't change that arrangement, though it did make the confines inside the vehicle when he joined them a little more snugly fitted.

Kimi sat facing him from the seat opposite him.

She made a point of looking out the side window, her fingers trailing up and down the cashmere scarf she'd wound around her neck. A long lock of silky hair had worked free of her chignon and clung to her ivory cheek.

He ignored the itch that made him long to slide his fingers through that lock.

Impartial, he reminded himself silently, for all the good that it did.

Other than Grace and an occasional word from Tanya, nobody seemed inclined to include Kimi in the desultory conversation that filled the short drive to the elementary school.

He was no better, though his problem was that he couldn't seem to stop watching her, while hunger sat, low and hot, inside him.

It annoyed the hell out of him, too—that lack of control.

He'd never felt particularly confounded by members of the

fairer sex. He'd shared their company—both in and out of bed—for half of his life, and he was no more immune to a beautiful woman than the next guy.

But he'd never been so damned disturbed by one, not even by Sydney James, and he'd been ready to marry her until she'd summarily dumped him. But not once could he recall thoughts of Sydney keeping him awake at night. She sure in hell had never distracted him from his work.

If it had ever come to a choice between her and his career, even at twenty-five, he'd known what he would choose.

Unlike Kimi, who stuck under the edge of his thoughts like a constant, little burr.

By the time they arrived at the school, he was as grateful as a caged animal to get out of the limo. Their car was met by the school's administrator, and after a round of bowing and introductions, they were escorted into the school's auditorium. It was already crowded with students and parents.

They took their places in the closely positioned seats. This time Greg was stuck next to Charity Smythe, and she leaned closer to him, as if they weren't already wedged in like sardines. "A group of us are going out after work this evening. A little celebration, actually. You're welcome to join us."

"Thanks, but I'll be making up for losing this afternoon."

"Well, maybe you'll change your mind."

He gave a noncommittal smile and contrarily wished that it were Kimi's warm body next to his.

The group of children had taken the stage, bearing their impressive collection of instruments, and Charity fell silent.

Fortunately, the children proved to be as spectacularly talented as they had been when he'd seen them playing a few months earlier at a fund-raiser in Tokyo, and Grace was more than pleased. "I now forgive you for making me schedule an unknown group," she patted his cheek with old familiarity, as they headed back toward the cars.

"They were just *wonderful*," Charity gushed. Once again, she'd managed to wedge herself next to Greg. He couldn't tell if she was flirting or sucking up to him. Either way, it left him unmoved. "When my sister and I were in school, we both played the oboe. Very difficult instrument, you know. What did you play in school?"

"Hooky." He thought he heard a muffled laugh come from Kimi, who was walking ahead of them.

He caught up to her at the car, feeling like some damn teenager who'd just earned an unexpected smile from the homecoming queen. "What about you? You went to elementary school in Tokyo?"

"Boarding school." She seemed willing—for the moment— to overlook their habit of butting heads as she looked back at the school.

Aside from the colorful posters hanging in the windows, the multistoried building looked to Greg just as institutional and indistinguishable as the cluster of businesses that flanked it. Even the shiny silver Christmas tree standing near the front was the same as the row of them marching down the street. If he hadn't already become accustomed to similar sights throughout Kyoto, he would have found it amazing that such modern structures could stand in such proximity to the temple that was across the street. It seemed to stand there, staring back at the interlopers in time with ancient patience.

"My school was the same one my father and his brother attended," Kimi added. The December breeze drifting over them was cold, and it lifted that loose lock of hair across her lips. "It was very different from this place. There were no posters at all there. No multiple stories. It was very traditional. The headmaster—" She broke off and shook her head slightly. "He was probably a credit to the boarding school, but as a child I found him unbearably stuffy. I sneaked away as often as I could, much to my father's dismay."

"Then I take it that you didn't miss the place when you left."

"No." She tucked the strands behind her ear. "I did not miss anything about Japan when we left." She gave him a sidelong look. "Are you shocked?"

"I didn't miss California when I finally left it behind. Should I be shocked?"

"Perhaps not." She was silent for a moment. "My father married Helen, and she changed our lives, for the better in every respect. Eventually we made our permanent home in Chicago. There were still private schools in my life, of course, but at least I was allowed to go home at the end of the day." She toyed with her neck scarf, standing aside while the others arranged themselves inside the limo. "What about you? I find the hooky line hard to believe. You look like the sort who earned top grades, ran the student body and was the fantasy of every tall, blond cheerleader."

"Not the brunettes?"

She rolled her eyes. "Them, as well. And the redheads and everything in between, I am certain."

"Believe the hooky part," he advised wryly. "By the time I left elementary school behind, earning good grades wasn't nearly as important to me as earning enough dough to keep me and Mona—my mother—off the streets." He ignored the shocked surprise in Kimi's eyes and took her hand to help her into the car. "After you, Ms. Taka."

He felt her fingers flex as if she wanted to draw away from his touch.

But she didn't.

She merely climbed in the car without further comment. She asked no more questions when they stopped at a ramen bar for lunch or when they rode back to the hotel again.

Maybe now that she had a hint of his background, she'd learned all she'd needed.

It had been as effective as hell with Sydney all those years ago. The second she'd learned how ignoble his beginnings were, she'd walked away and never looked back.

When they arrived at the hotel, there was a limousine parked in front. The vehicle wasn't one of the hotel's fleet, and he studied it curiously as he waited by the car for the women to alight.

But when Kimi stepped out onto the sidewalk and eyed the elderly Japanese couple exiting the other vehicle, he felt her sigh. "I should have known," he heard her murmur.

He looked again at the car. The couple was eyeing them and Kimi put a strained-looking smile on her face. "My grandparents," she told him, and headed toward the couple.

The woman was shorter than Kimi, and she hugged her, clearly delighted. Even Kimi's grandfather looked pleased, though his greeting was considerably more circumspect.

What Greg was noticing more, however, was the subdued manner Kimi displayed around her grandparents.

He walked over to join them. *"Konichiwa."*

Kimi gave him a decidedly grateful look at the interruption and quickly launched into introductions.

Greg bowed again and presented Kimi's grandfather with the business card he'd pulled out. *"Dōzo yoroshiku.* It is an honor to meet you both. I understand that I owe you my gratitude for the encouragement you extended Kobayashi-san to attend our luncheon yesterday."

Yukio Taka tilted his iron-gray head, accepting the card with the gravity that Greg had only found here in Japan. "It was my pleasure to assist." Yukio's English was gruff but smooth. He looked up at the hotel soaring above their heads. His expression was hard to decipher. "I have seen TAKA on many buildings, but I am still surprised to see the name on a hotel. This is what has happened when my son married a gaijin."

"You have learned great respect for Helen, *O-jii-san,*" Kimi reminded. "Taka hotels will be among the best in the world."

He made a low "hmm" that didn't sound particularly convinced, but he didn't argue outright.

"You will please to forgive us for interrupting your day?" Kimi's grandmother asked in a soft, lilting voice. "I could wait no longer to see my Kimi-chan again." She kept Kimi's hand clasped between hers.

"Oba-chan," Kimi protested, "I saw you just a few days ago."

Her grandmother made a dismissing sound that transcended language. "For too brief a time. We were too rushed to…what do you say? Catch up all the way. I wish to see you here in this place where you say that you are doing your work."

"Naturally. If you'll excuse me," Greg said, "I'll leave you to enjoy one another's company. I apologize for our unfinished state, but I'm certain that your granddaughter will give you an admirable tour." Another round of bowing ensued before he left them. The hint of abandonment in Kimi's eyes went with him.

Grace and the others had already disappeared into the hotel, and the second he showed his face through the lobby doors, he was accosted by half a dozen people, and the wave didn't stop even after he finally made it down to his office.

That didn't stop him from noticing, however, when Kimi walked by hours later.

Alone.

He went to the door of his office. "Ms. Taka."

She looked back at him. "Yes?"

Most of the workers on the floor had long departed for the day. "What are you doing down here?"

She hitched the cardboard box she was holding higher in her arms. "Finishing an internal mailing about the staff holiday party that Grace wants out by tomorrow."

Grace, he knew, had also left for the day. Kimi looked braced for him to crack down on her again for some imagined sin.

He hid a sigh. "Where are your grandparents?"

"No favor goes unpunished. They are dining with Mr. and

Mrs. Kobayashi this evening. Their trip here was not simply to see their disgraceful granddaughter in her new job. They have to repay the price of Kobayashi's favor to them."

"Give me that." He took the heavy box from her and headed down the corridor toward sales. "Your grandparents don't think you're disgraceful." If anything they'd looked typically doting.

He'd never known his grandparents—doting or otherwise. For that matter, he'd never known his father.

"Maybe my grandmother does not find me to be." She trailed after him. "My grandfather is another story. But he blames much of my willful ways on my father for not having married me off by now in some advantageously designed match. He is thoroughly dismayed that instead of being truly useful, I am being allowed to play around in the family business." She held open the department's smoked-glass door so he could carry the box through. "If it were not for Helen's influence, I think an arranged marriage is exactly what my father would be most happy to do."

"I've met your father. He doesn't strike me as holding that deeply to old customs."

She swiped her hand at that still-loose lock of hair, but it drifted back to tease the gentle point of her chin. "At one time he did. And then he met Helen and didn't seem to mind causing his own piece of scandal. My grandfather even wanted to take back the running of TAKA from him when he realized my father was interested in Helen on more than just a business level, though he reconsidered. My mother—my real mother—and my father had an arranged marriage. Considering the way she ended up, she was no happier with the match than he was. She just took a coward's way out."

He set the box on the space she cleared for him on top of her desk. "I'm sorry."

She studied him for a moment. "I actually believe you mean that."

"Surprise, surprise," he murmured. "A heart beats inside me, after all."

"I would not presume otherwise," she offered with undue politeness, then pressed her lips softly together as if to prevent them from revealing the real truth.

He dragged his gaze from her mouth. "Do you remember your mother?"

"Only from her pictures. I look like her. Maybe that is why it is so easy for some in my family to expect the worst of me." She flipped open the box and began pulling out banded-together packs of colorful flyers.

"Whereas I don't have that excuse," he concluded. He pinched the bridge of his nose. "Again, I apologize. I jumped to conclusions."

"Forget it." She didn't look at him as she turned to the cabinets against the wall. "There is no denying that I have pulled some foolish stunts along the way." She dumped the box of envelopes she'd pulled out alongside the flyers.

"You haven't since you arrived here."

"I have been here little more than a week." She gave him a breezy look that he wouldn't have bought even if he hadn't seen the sheen in her eyes. "Give it time," she advised.

"Kimi."

She dragged another packet out of the box and sat down behind her desk. "If you're going to just stand there, I could use another box of these envelopes."

He silently found another box and set it on top of the first but caught her hands in his, stopping her movements. "What's really going on here?"

She tugged her hands free. *"Nothing."* But she suddenly propped her elbows on her desk and pressed her forehead to her hands. "I came here wanting things to be different than they had been at college."

"How were things at college?"

"It does not matter," she whispered.

"From where I'm standing, it looks like it matters a lot."

She straightened, dashing her hands across her cheeks. "Everyone in my family is successful. I suppose you know that."

Unless a person lived under a rock, it was hard not to. Despite the hitches that her family encountered in business or in their personal lives—hitches that had more often than not been recounted in the media in one way or another—the Hansons and the Takas seemed to end up turning the hitch into golden success. "Yes, I know that."

"Everyone but me."

"You're young."

"Do not remind me."

"There's no point in forgetting it," he said quietly. "It doesn't mean you're not capable of attaining your own success. But even for people like you, it takes some time."

"People like me." She looked pained. "I almost feel it would be easier if I thought you were referring to my culture, but I know you are not. If anything, you are more in tune with the Japanese than I am. Sue—I do not even know her last name, but I met her that first day at the staff meeting—"

"—Huang," he provided.

Her lips lifted a little. "Of course you would know. She likened the staff here to the United Nations, and she was right. You treat everyone fairly and with great respect."

"Not everyone."

She ducked her chin and looked away. "You want what is best for the Taka. I realize that you do not necessarily think that my involvement here furthers that goal. I am the only one working within these walls who does not meet even your basic criteria of qualifications. Three years of work experience in a first-class hotel, is it not?"

He didn't deny it. If she didn't have the pedigree that she did, she would never have made it through the doors as an employee.

"You have a qualification that others don't. You're a Taka. This—" he waved his hand over their head "—is a Taka hotel."

"Which brings us back to *people like me*."

"I meant people raised in wealth."

"Yes. I know." She was obviously making an effort to shake off her troubled thoughts. "And I suppose I only proved my naïveté when I thought that things would be different here than they had been at school."

He bent his knees, crouching down beside her chair, and swiveled it around until he could see her face. "Different how?"

She was silent for a long moment. "Do you know where the rest of the department is?" she finally asked.

"No."

"They are all out celebrating Charity's birthday." She looked down at her hands. "Everyone but me."

So that was Charity's little celebration. "You could have gone if you'd wanted."

"I was not asked," she elaborated, as if he didn't understand the finer points of the matter. "And believe me. I *know* how pathetic that sounds."

"You want to fit in."

Her lips twisted. "And as you so plainly told me, I will never really be part of—" her fingers sketched out quotation marks "—the family."

"I'm sorry."

"For being truthful?"

He covered her fingers with one hand. "Because I know how hard it can be to fit in."

Her lashes lifted. "When have you ever *not* fit in?"

He couldn't help himself.

He brushed the stray lock of hair away from her cheek. The hair was as silky as he'd suspected. The cheek as satiny and cool.

"Plenty of times," he admitted. Most of the time. Even here at the Taka was no exception.

It didn't seem possible, but her eyes darkened even more. She sucked in her lower lip for a moment, then softly let out a breath.

His gaze dropped to the faint gleam she left behind on that soft, pink mouth. He felt her fingers move beneath his palm to thread, ever so slowly between his.

"Kimi." Damn it to hell, he was losing his mind. "Ms. Taka—"

She leaned closer. "Mr. Sherman." Her voice was little more than a whisper across his chin.

"Oh! I didn't realize anyone was here."

Greg yanked back at the intrusion of a third voice. He looked past Kimi to see Grace eyeing them.

Kimi's cheeks flushed, and she quickly snatched up another flyer to shove into an envelope.

"I thought you'd left for the day," he told Grace.

"I came back for this." She lifted her briefcase. "Kimi, dear, I think the mailing can wait until morning." There was no mistaking her meaning.

She was sending Kimi out.

Kimi still gave him a quick glance before she slid out of her chair and pushed it neatly beneath the desk. She passed Grace. "Good night, Grace. Mr. Sherman."

Greg watched until she'd slipped out the smoked door.

"What the hell are you doing, Greg?" Grace's voice finally broke the strained quiet left between them.

He raked his hand down his face. "Not now, Grace." He brushed past her and left the office, too.

Not because she had no business asking the question of him. They went back way too far for that.

But because he didn't know how to answer.

No matter which way he looked at it, Kimi Taka was off limits, and he'd better start remembering it.

Chapter Seven

Kimi was still shaking after she made it up to the twenty-first floor.

She practically ran down the hall to her room and fumbled the key out of her pocket only to realize that the traditional lock had been removed.

In its place was an electronic model.

For which she would need a key card.

She pressed her palms against the door for a moment and drew in several long, calming breaths.

There was still no one working in reception. With no guests to receive, yet, there was no need. She could go find Greg, she knew, and he would be able to cut a key card for her. Common sense, however, told her that she would be better off—*safer*, that annoying voice inside her head whispered—visiting the security office. As she well knew, guests or not, it was already being staffed twenty-four hours a day, seven days a week.

Thank heavens Grace had interrupted them before Kimi had succeeded in making a monstrously huge fool of herself.

She could not believe how close she had come to pressing her mouth against his.

Could not believe how desperately she had wanted to.

Greg Sherman was the last person with whom she needed to complicate her life. She kept telling herself that, yet didn't seem to get any further along in believing it.

She was an adult. Or at least she was supposed to be proving that particular fact. Getting involved with Greg—no matter how tempting—was simply out of the question.

She was in Kyoto to work.

Not to be caught dallying with the boss!

She blew out a shaking breath, ran her sweating palms down the sides of her salmon suit and turned on her heel.

At the wholly unexpected sight of Greg, however, the oversized brass key fell from her nerveless fingers, and her feet suddenly felt rooted in place. "Greg." He was already halfway up the hall toward her. "I did not...not hear the elevator."

"I came up the service elevator."

Of course he had. Never to cross the line between employee of the hotel and guest of the hotel.

While she—intentionally or not—was straddling the line of both, and at this point not feeling particularly successful at either.

He stopped several circumspect feet away, but she could still see the way a muscle ticked unevenly in the hard line of his jaw. What she could not see, however, were his thoughts.

They were too well hidden behind his shuttered green eyes.

"We should talk." His voice seemed even deeper than usual.

She lifted her hand. "Stop. Please, no talk. I...I crossed a line that I never should—" she inhaled quickly "—have crossed."

"You?" He took a step closer, only to stop and drag his tie another inch looser. "What happened—nearly happened was—"

"—just a moment," she inserted hastily. "Nothing more than that."

"It was a *moment*—" his voice dragged over the word "—that we can't repeat."

"Do you think I do not know that?" She pressed her hands to her hot cheeks. "Even *I* am aware that throwing myself at you is inappropriate!"

He let out a harsh breath. "You didn't do anything inappropriate. I'm the one who can't seem to keep from wanting you."

Everything inside her jolted to a standstill as his words settled over her. Then, with an unsteady jerk, her heart tripped back into rapid action. Her shoe slid forward. "Greg—"

"Stick with Mr. Sherman," he said roughly. "We're both safer."

She gave a jerky nod. "Of course, you're right. Mr. Sherman."

"Okay." He flipped his hand down his tie. "Good night then, Ms. Taka."

He turned on his heel, striding back down the hall with unmistakable finality.

Protest screamed through her, and she actually took another thoughtless step after him before she managed to rein in the impulse. But then she noticed the key she had dropped on the carpet.

She quickly picked it up and hurried after him. "Wait. I need a key card." She held out the brass key when he looked back at her. "The lock was changed today."

"You should have been given a card, already." Without touching her fingers, he plucked the key from her. "I'll get it sent up to you immediately."

"I could just go down with—no." Staying away from confining spaces with him was probably wise. "I will wait up here. Thank you."

He gave a faint nod and walked away.

Kimi had paced the long corridor several times over when Shin Endo arrived bearing the key card.

She told herself that it was her imagination that the man gave her a knowing look in the moment it took to hand over the key and depart again. It wasn't as if she expected Grace to start off a spate of gossip about what she had very nearly seen.

Kimi's supervisor had *seen* nothing, anyway, because nothing had happened.

The jittering inside her gave lie to that as she went into her suite where the message light on her telephone was blinking. The message was from Helen, warning her that her grandparents had mentioned dropping by to see Kimi.

"Too late." Kimi erased the message. She would call Helen in the morning when it would be a more reasonable hour in Chicago.

There were class assignments that she needed to work on, but instead of settling in front of her computer, she found herself wandering around the spacious suite. From the windows overlooking the twinkle of lights outside the hotel, beyond the infinitely patient computer, to the wide, turned-down bed complete with a mint on the pillow.

She realized she did not even know who had been cleaning her room.

She had occupied the suite for more than a week. Each day when she returned from her duties, the rooms were clean. Fresh flowers were placed in the vases scattered around the lovely tables. The clothes that she had left laying in a heap on her bedroom floor showed up laundered and pressed and hanging in her closet.

Was it any wonder that most of the employees there found it hard to accept her as one of "them"?

First thing she was going to do the next day was make arrangements to move *out* of the Mahogany Suite.

If she wanted people to look beyond the name of Taka, then she had better start showing them there really was more to her than the name. And that went beyond filling water glasses at a banquet or stuffing envelopes.

She resolutely ignored the whisper inside her that warned the approval of the person that was becoming most important to her lately had little to do with her job, at all.

"Are you sure you don't want me to come in?"

Greg looked at the invitation in Sondra Fleming's eyes. Not only had she been willing to accompany him to a business dinner that evening on only a few hours notice when he hadn't bothered to call her even once over the past several weeks, but she was obviously interested in extending the evening into much more personal hours.

She was sexy and intelligent and even though he'd enjoyed spending time sharing her bed before, Greg now couldn't summon the slightest interest.

Maybe he needed those herbs of his mother's after all.

He put some regret into his smile. "I have another middle-of-the-night conference call and an early-morning breakfast meeting." The excuses were true enough.

She pouted lightly. "On a Saturday?"

"Time's drawing short before our first guests check in," he reminded. "There won't be any Saturdays off for me for some time."

"I suppose not. Don't wait so long to call me next time, though, darling. My schedule might not be so readily available."

"Much to my loss," he assured smoothly. "Good night, Sondra."

She leaned forward and pressed her mouth to his before he could climb out of the limo. Then she leaned back, looking satisfied. "Good night, darling."

Greg climbed out into the cold night air, closed the limo door, and the sleek car smoothly moved away from the curb. He let out a long breath. Thank God women just didn't get it that when a man really wanted to get horizontal with her, late night conference calls and early morning meetings didn't get in the way.

"*Kombanwa*, Sherman-san." Johnny Ito, the security officer on duty pulled open the lobby door when Greg reached it.

"Good evening, Johnny. Everything quiet?"

"*Hai.*" Johnny deftly locked the doors once more. "I will enjoy it while it lasts," he admitted. "Next week the hotel will be alive with guests, and quiet will be a thing of the past."

"Let's hope so. That's what keeps our paychecks coming."

Johnny grinned, and Greg strode across the newly laid floor. For once he didn't head down to his office but took the elevator up to his room.

But the sight of Kimi Taka stopped him before he reached his room. She was barefoot and wearing a pink sweat suit with a waist-length top that didn't come close to meeting the waist of the pants clinging low enough over her slender hips to reveal a small, glittering diamond in her navel.

She looked no less startled, though her lashes swiftly fell, hiding her expressive eyes from him. "Hello."

It was their encounter the prior evening that had spurred him into calling Sondra. For all the good that had done in helping him forget it. He definitely didn't need to be thinking about it now with just the two of them standing within feet of his room.

He'd never particularly understood the appeal of a pierced navel before, but there was something expressly distracting about the stone that glittered against Kimi's smooth skin, and he dragged his attention from it, only to get hung up along the way on the lush curves of her soft mouth.

Swearing inwardly at himself, he looked down at her bare feet, ignoring the curiosity of the ice bucket held against her midriff. "Where are your shoes?"

She looked down at her bright pink-painted toes, wriggling them against the carpet. "In my room. I did not expect to run into anyone."

Which hardly explained why her shoes were in her room, yet she was down here on this floor. His floor.

He gestured toward the filled bronze bucket, diligently refraining from eyeing that little shining stone just below the hem of her pink sweatshirt. "You could call for ice, you know. Or there are the machines actually *on* your floor."

"I know."

Something was off, and it wasn't just her shoes.

There were only three rooms in use in the hotel. Her suite on twenty-one. His room behind him and Shin's room across the hall and around the corner. "Do you play poker?"

Her lashes lifted at that. "Poker? No. Why?"

Because Greg had excused himself from the game in order to attend the dinner. Which had left at least two open seats at the table, since he knew that Grace had been in Tokyo for the day courting the planners of an international jewelry expo. "No reason."

Kimi's fine brows twitched together over her nose. "Hmm. Well, good night."

"Good night." But he didn't move toward his room.

She didn't head toward the elevator.

He gave her a close look. "What's going on?"

She lifted her chin a little. "Nothing."

"Right." He slowly closed the distance between them. "That's why you're more than a dozen floors away from home."

"Chicago is a lot farther away than that."

"Kimi—"

"I thought we had agreed on the Ms. Taka, Mr. Sherman route."

His teeth closed together. *"Kimi."*

"Oh, all right. If you are going to make such a big deal about it. I just moved out of the Mahogany Suite after work today," she announced with studied casualness. "That is all."

He suspected the answer to come, but the pained awareness inside him forced him to ask, anyway. "To...where?"

"A standard room on this floor. Obviously."

He scrubbed his hand down his face. "And you did this because…?" Because she wanted to torment him just a little more?

"Because I never should have been in the Mahogany Suite in the first place." She switched the insulated bucket from one arm to the other and pinned him with a suddenly accusing look. "*You* should never have stuck me up there."

"You're blaming me for putting you, the owner's daughter, in one of our best suites?"

"I am staff." Her voice was carefully dignified. "I should be treated like the other staff living on-site."

She should be placed far, far away—like the twenty-first floor far away—if only for his peace of mind. That peace involved even more than his fairly basic desire to keep his career from blowing up in his face. "Kimi, you can surely see that this isn't a good idea."

Her chin lifted another notch. "Why? I checked reservations, you know. And I saw what you did. Ambassador and Mrs. Diggins are arriving next week. They were supposed to have the Mahogany Suite, but you switched their reservation to the Ginger Suite when I arrived."

"The Ginger Suite is almost identical to yours."

"It is not *mine*. Mrs. Diggins specifically requested the Mahogany Suite. What were you going to tell them when they arrived? That they could not have the suite they desired because spoiled Kimi Taka was in the house?" She shook her head, and her long hair rippled over her shoulders. "No, thank you."

"Honey, I've been pacifying the expectations of demanding guests since you were drinking milk and eating graham crackers in elementary school. I wasn't worried about the ambassador and his supercilious wife."

"No, you were worried about keeping the boss's daughter pampered, so she did not go complaining to her parents and make your life here even more uncomfortable. My father and Helen are prone to indulging me, Greg, but I can assure you that I would never be able to influence their business decisions in that way."

He couldn't afford to believe that particular point. "If you don't want the Mahogany, then *you* can use the Ginger Suite."

Instead of looking annoyed, though, she just tilted her head and gave him a searching look. "If I did not know better, I would think you were afraid of having me so close at hand."

"The twenty-first floor has extra layers of security."

Her lips stretched into a sudden smile. "Oh. This is about *my* security, then?" She shook her head. "I might still remember the taste of those graham crackers and milk, *honey*, but I am not that young." She padded silently past him, stopping at the door—damn it all to hell—immediately next to his and, with a nudge of her slender hip, pushed the unlatched door open. "And by the way, Greg? If you are going to be indulging in late-night parties, I would appreciate it if you could keep it down."

He followed on her heels, right through the doorway. "What's that supposed to mean?"

She set the ice bucket down on the desk that was an exact duplicate of the one in his own room and plucked a tissue from the box sitting atop a thick stack of books.

Then she stepped up to him and damned if he didn't have to consciously hold his place when she reached up and dabbed the tissue against the corner of his mouth. "You tell me." Her voice thinned as she held up the tissue. A deep red lipstick smudge stained it. "I would have not suspected that this was your color, but then you are often full of surprises."

He grabbed the tissue from her and rubbed it harder across his mouth, removing any vestiges of Sondra's lipstick. "You can't be next door to me."

Her smile looked demure, but beneath, he suspected it was really full of the devil. "Afraid your other women might get the wrong idea?"

He crumpled the tissue and tossed it aside. "There are no women."

"So the lipstick *is* actually yours." She waited a mocking beat. "You know, you think you know a guy—"

"Cut it out. Do you know what sort of gossip this is going to create?"

"That the he-man macho Greg Sherman wears lipstick when he is off duty?"

"What's the matter, Kimi? Are you jealous that I was with another woman this evening?"

Her mocking sarcasm fell by the wayside. "And if I am?" Her hands lifted at her sides and fell again. "There is nothing to be done about it. You have made that abundantly clear." She crossed the room and stared out the window that he knew provided a stellar view of absolutely nothing.

Which was why these particular rooms made excellent staff quarters. No guest would be likely to want the location.

Yet Kimi had chosen it. The one room with a less desirable location than even his own.

He eyed the perfectly formed line of her profile, outlined by the void beyond the window. A profile that had been haunting his sleep since the day she'd dumped her mountain of luggage in his lobby.

The mountain that was now piled precariously in the corner of the room, obviously in the process of being unpacked yet again.

He walked over to the closed door on the other side of the queen-sized bed. It was the one of the few differences between the furnishings in this room and his.

He had a larger bed.

Which was the last thing he needed to be thinking about.

He rattled the doorknob on the door. "Do you know what this is?"

She gave a flicking glance. "Yes."

"Connecting doors, Kimi. Do you really want everyone who works here to know that you and I are in connecting rooms?"

"Maybe you just do not want that knowledge to make it back to my parents."

"I don't," he confirmed swiftly. "Hospitality is a bloody small world, and the last thing I need is for anyone to start thinking I've gotten where I am here at the Taka by riding on your very sexy coattails."

"That is ridiculous. Helen had already hired you long before I came on the scene."

"A detail that will be easily forgotten in most minds, I guarantee."

She gave him a sidelong look. "So what you really are worried about is not my reputation, but yours."

He turned the knob and threw open the door so hard it banged against the wall. He stopped it from bouncing shut again with the flat of his hand, leaving visible the opposing door that was locked from his room on the other side. "What I'm worried about," he said flatly, "is that it's going to be too damned easy for us to pull these doors open and damn the consequences."

She finally looked shaken.

And impossibly vulnerable.

It was a look that he was coming to recognize on her face more than he would ever have expected, and he was no more immune to it now than he was the first time he'd seen past her glossy exterior that night in Sakura.

"What about the woman whose lipstick you wear?" Her voice was quietly distinct.

He shouldn't have followed her into her room.

It was too damned close.

Too damned intimate.

He knew just how easy it would be to put his hands on her, and taking the direct line from that point A to the queen-sized point B with the pillows that she'd already tousled around would be even easier. "If I were a smart man—" he looked away from the bed "—I'd be with her right now."

She looked pained. The muscles of her ivory throat worked in a hard swallow. "Then why are you not?"

"Because I draw the line at making love to one woman while thinking about another!"

Her lips parted. Sudden color rode the high arch of her cheeks. "Oh, Greg." It was little more than a sigh, but it still went straight to his gut.

"Move back to the twenty-first floor," he advised roughly. "We'll both be safer."

"I do not wish to move back up there." She moistened her lips and pressed her hands down her thighs. "Nor do I wish to cause more…dissension between us. But working here at the Taka is something I have to do, Greg. And I have to do it correctly. Please try to understand that."

"Why? You don't have to prove anything, Kimi. For God's sake, you could swing the world by its tail if you so choose."

"You mean because I am a Taka. Do you not see? What is it worth to gain something simply because of my family's name? This was the same problem I had at university!"

"If you *had* no family name, you might have a different opinion."

Kimi stared at Greg, frowning. "You cannot be referring to yourself. Look where you are. You are head of a world-class hotel."

"I *work* for a world-class hotel," he said evenly. "I am well aware how easily that particular fact can change."

"Not because of me."

"Exactly because of you. Go back to the suite, Kimi. For all of our sakes."

She shook her head. "No."

He raked his hands through his hair, looking thoroughly aggravated. "Why the hell not?"

"I want to prove that I matter, all right?" Kimi's words rang through the room, seeming to hang in place, utterly out of her reach and beyond her ability to take them back.

Greg's eyes narrowed. He slowly closed the space between them, not stopping until he was inches away and sucking up the oxygen her brain cells needed for reasonable function. "Of course you matter. Your family—"

"—loves me." She could not back up because the window was behind her. Nor could she sidestep, because the very fashionable and very functional dark wood desk covered with her laptop and the textbooks she badly wished to cover up was at her side.

Standard rooms in the hotel were unquestionably beautifully appointed, but they were a fraction of the size of the suite she had thoughtlessly occupied.

"I know they do. And I know I am making no sense, so please forget I said anything." She bravely stepped forward to slip around him, but ruined the effect by catching her breath when their bodies brushed even briefly. *"Sumimasen."* She stole a glance at him through her lashes.

He cursed softly, and suddenly slid his hand around her waist, pulling her back against him.

Her heartbeat stuttered, then raced. Her hands pressed against the lapels of his beautifully tailored black suit jacket and just as quickly pulled away. But not even closing them in a fist against her middle could erase the heat they had felt. "Mr. Sherman."

"Too late," he said huskily, and pressed his mouth against hers.

He tasted of coffee. A hint of sake. Then even the slightest hint of objectivity was beyond her because the only thing she could grasp were his arms. Then his shoulders. And she did not need the iron band of his arm around her back to press her closer, because there *was* no closer. His breath was her breath. His pulse was her pulse.

But just as abruptly, he lifted his head, and pushed her at

arms' length, holding on to her shoulders, which was a good thing because her legs seemed incapable of normal function.

He was hauling in deep breaths as if he had just run a marathon, and she vaguely realized that she was in no better condition.

"Please do not say that we shouldn't have done that," she managed breathlessly.

"Not voicing the words doesn't make them any less true." His jaw canted to one side, then centered again. His hands slowly fell away from her shoulders, leaving her feeling chilled despite the heat still bubbling through her veins.

Her knees were still too weak to be of use, and she sank down onto the edge of the bed. "We are the only ones who know what occurs in this room."

"Go ahead and keep trying to believe that." His voice was low. Deep. It slid over her, warm and enveloping. "I've been in this business too long to not know better. There *are* no secrets in hotels, Kimi."

"But—"

"Do up your zipper."

Her mouth closed. She looked down, oddly startled to realize that the zip on her hoodie was halfway down her chest, showing him most clearly by the narrow strip of nude flesh that she wore nothing at all beneath it.

She fumbled with the tab, and if she had managed to keep from looking at him, she never would have hesitated. She would have yanked the zipper right up to her throat.

But she did glance at him.

She did see the fierce flame that made the pale green in his eyes look more like gold. She did see the way his knuckles looked white as he dragged at the knot of his paisley tie.

Her heart skipped around, and her nipples tightened even more, achingly sensitive against the soft fleece. What would he do if she drew the zipper all the way down?

The heady answer was there in his taut face.

"Up, Kimi," he said, obviously reading her mind. "This might be routine for you, but I'm not ready to jeopardize an entire career again because my willpower where you're concerned is seriously AWOL."

Again? "But it is not routine." She yanked the zipper up and pressed her hands down against the bed, her fingers digging into the thick downy bedding. "I am not...I mean, I have not—"

"Slept with the boss before? That's not difficult since we both know this is the first job you've ever had."

"What did you mean by *again*?"

"Let's just say that this is not the first time a rich little girl has screwed with the help."

She swallowed hard. "Did you l-love her?"

"I don't love anyone but my hotels." He turned away and finished yanking off his tie, only to twist the patterned silk around his fist.

She wondered if he was imagining it to be a noose around someone's neck. His? Or hers?

She bit down on her tongue, rather than make the situation even worse. When she felt certain that she would not blurt out the truth about just how *un*-routine this sort of thing was for her, she pushed off the bed and forced herself into a steady pace to the room's main door. She turned back to face him, but looked no higher than the hard rise of his tanned throat above the snowy white shirt collar. "If you prefer, I will find accommodations at another establishment. But I will not go back to using a room here that has not been set aside for staff."

"Staying in another hotel is out of the question." He grimaced. "That would make great press coverage, wouldn't it? Kimiko Taka doesn't even want to stay in the same hotel that shares her name."

Irritation nuzzled against the desire still swamping her. "What would you have me do then, Greg? You don't want me on the same floor as you, and you don't want me to leave altogether. You would prefer me to occupy that premium suite at the expense of the very service we are supposed to offer our guests, and then you could continue believing that I am just the selfishly pampered heiress whose playacting at a job does not even merit a proper employee badge?"

"I don't think that."

"But you did when I arrived here."

"And I was wrong," he said flatly. "Which I've admitted. And picking an argument doesn't make this—" his hand waved in a brief motion between them "—*whatever* the hell it is between us just disappear."

The fact that he wanted *whatever* to disappear was more than plain.

Kimi knew that she had been blessed with more than her fair share of pride. It was that overabundant trait that had caused all manner of misbehaviors on her part in the past. But right now, that pride was painfully elusive.

She clasped the door handle behind her back. "Then what do you suggest?"

"Damned if I know," he muttered. He reached around her and opened the door himself. "You do your job and stay out of my hair, and I'll do the same. Deal?"

She pressed her lips tightly together and managed a nod.

He did not look overly convinced or thrilled.

But he did step out of her room and she quickly shut the door. Then she followed that up by turning the security lock, as well.

"Good girl," she heard him say through the door.

She let out a long sigh and moved away from the door, only to be faced with the still-open connecting door.

Moistening her lips, she sat on the side of the bed, staring at it. Knowing she should close it.

Praying that he would open the other door from his side.

"This one, too, Kimi." From his room on the other side,

Greg's voice was muffled but distinct enough. The second door remained firmly closed.

She bounced off the bed and slammed her connecting door shut.

With it safely locked between them, she slid her back down it until she sat on the floor. Drawing up her legs, she pressed her forehead to her knees.

But it was a very long time before she stopped trembling.

Chapter Eight

Getting through the weekend without running into Greg was not as difficult as Kimi expected it to be. Not when she remained entirely in her room, venturing out only to meet with Chef Lorenzo and Anton Tessier to discuss another menu change for the Nguyen's wedding reception and to sneak in a kitchen raid when she could no longer ignore her hunger pangs.

The rest of the time she had spent figuring out what to do with her overabundance of clothing and luggage since the closet space in her new accommodations was considerably less accommodating than the suite had been, and gathering research for the last paper she needed to write before the semester ended that week.

When she finally left behind the room for work on Monday morning, she knew that Greg had already left his room much earlier. She was painfully attuned to any noises from his room, but the only thing she had been able to hear was the muffled sound of his door opening and closing.

The service elevators were even busier than usual, so Kimi took the stairs, stopping off at the lobby level to return the key card for the Mahogany Suite; something she had forgotten to do amid the task of moving out of it before the weekend.

It was plainly evident just from the heightened energy and activity in the hotel that they were rapidly gearing toward receiving their first guests the following day.

If she had not personally witnessed the effort that had gone into the transformation of the lobby from its unfinished state when she had first arrived to its current completed luxury, she would have thought that magic had been at play.

Gone were the pallets of marble and wood. Metal scaffolding no longer crisscrossed the high, faintly golden-toned walls. The fountain, presently flanked by magnificent holiday poinsettias fashioned into tall Christmas "trees", was a soothing focal point for all who would enter the lobby, and particularly for those who chose to relax in the deceptive comfort of the low couches and chairs arranged between it and the soaring windows that overlooked the most traditional of the various gardens the hotel boasted.

There were pristinely attired men and women behind the reception desk that was elegantly decked with boughs of berry-sprigged garland, and even the uniformed doormen were in place.

It struck Kimi as oddly surreal.

A busy, beautifully constructed, elegant and sophisticatedly appointed building, just holding its breath as it awaited the guests that would truly bring it to life as a world-class hotel.

She spotted Greg talking with an auburn-haired woman behind reception and made herself continue to the desk in a natural fashion, aiming for the clerk—ponytailed Sue—who stood farthest from Greg.

"You're leaving?" Sue asked when Kimi handed over the card to her. She looked just as disconcerted by Kimi's presence as she had when she had learned who Kimi was at that first staff meeting.

"No." Evidently the details of her move out of the suite had not yet traveled entirely along the hotel grapevine. Kimi hoped that meant her presence at the Taka was no longer such a novelty. "I switched rooms last week and neglected to return this key." From the corner of her eye she could see Greg and the redhead.

"What other room could you possibly want? Next to the Presidential Suite, the Mahogany is the best we have." Her eyes widened. "Did you move up *there*?"

"Oh, no," Kimi assured quickly. "I am just down on four where Gr—Mr. Sherman and Mr. Endo also stay."

Something in Sue's surprised expression shifted, and Kimi wished that she had not said anything at all. She quickly wished Sue good luck for the following day and excused herself.

Employees were still arriving when Kimi made it down to her department. She could see Grace sitting at her desk as she passed by her office. Thankfully, the other woman merely offered an absent "Good morning" and refrained from commenting about the last time she had seen Kimi with Greg.

Relieved, because she really had not known what to expect from her supervisor, Kimi returned the greeting and quickly went through to the main office. The coffeemaker was cold and empty and she rapidly started a pot.

Before long, Tanya arrived, seeming to bring in cold air with her as she unwound her scarf and shrugged out of her coat. "Oh, you're a peach. Coffee. It is really cold outside."

Kimi poured a mug and handed it to the shivering girl. "I have not been out," she admitted.

Tanya cradled the mug in her hands. "Why would you want to? If I got to live here, I wouldn't be out there, either." There did not seem to be any judgment or envy in her voice, though. Just wry humor and a chattiness that had been present only since they had both pitched in to help with the mayor's luncheon. "There's actually snow in the forecast for the next few weeks. Charity will have a litter of puppies if it actually hits. She chairs the committee that runs the staff holiday party," Tanya added.

Realization dawned on Kimi. She had stuffed so many envelopes with the save-the-date flyer that she now felt slow on the uptake. "I didn't realize the details of the party had already been determined."

"They haven't. But Charity figures that since she chairs the committee, her idea to have it in Sakura and the rooftop garden will override anyone else's ideas. But there's no way the party'll be on the roof if it's snowing, because we can't all fit in just the restaurant." Tanya looked a tiny bit gleeful about the prospect.

"Don't even *suggest* snow." Charity's voice accosted them as she entered the room. She glared at Tanya as if the girl were Mother Nature in disguise. "Outdoor heaters were invented for a reason, and I can bring in plenty for the party no matter how cold it gets. It will be a winter wonderland," she assured.

Tanya shrugged and headed toward her desk, but she slid a mischievous glance toward Kimi along the way. "Icy and appropriate," she whispered. Kimi could not help but grin back at her.

Then the rest of their coworkers seemed to arrive en masse, and the workday was off to a bustling start. The pace didn't slow until late that afternoon when Grace shooed everyone up to the training room for a last staff meeting before the big "O".

"Occupancy day," Tanya provided to Kimi as they trooped out and went up to the fifth floor. She lowered her voice again, looking rueful. "For some of us, that big 'O' is the only orgasmic thing going on in our lives at all."

Kimi felt her face flush and was grateful that Tanya's attention had turned ahead once again.

When they arrived, the training room was considerably more crowded than it had been the first day of Kimi's arrival, and she slid in to stand at the back of the room alongside Tanya and Nigel.

The redhead she had seen that morning with Greg was at the front of the room along with the rest of the senior management.

She leaned toward Tanya. "Who is the woman next to Mr. Sherman?"

"Bridget McElroy. I guess she's over the flu by now. She's Mr. Sherman's administrative assistant." Tanya made a slight face.

"You don't like her?"

Tanya tilted her head toward Kimi's and lowered her voice even more. "She's okay. But I heard they're sleeping together."

Kimi jerked. "What? Heard from whom?"

Tanya shrugged. "Oh, you know. Word travels, particularly through hotels. Who can blame her? Most of the women—single or not—who work for the man would jump at that chance. He's handsome, successful and I hear he earns a fortune. And he *did* bring her with him when he came to the Taka."

"He chose a lot of people to come to the Taka," Kimi pointed out, striving for a normal tone.

"Well, whatever. She won't get anywhere with him in the end. Charity knows someone he was involved with in Germany. Absolutely crazy for him, but he walked away without a second glance when he got the position here at the Taka."

Fortunately, Greg stepped to the front of the room and immediately drew everyone's attention, so the subject was dropped.

Unfortunately, however, a good portion of the meeting went in one ear and right out the other because Kimi could not manage to concentrate on anything other than watching for some sign between Greg and Bridget that supported Tanya's rumors.

Considering Kimi's experience with Greg, she wanted to doubt it.

But really, how would she know?

Just because Greg had a host of intractable reasons why he wanted to keep *her* at a distance didn't mean he applied those reasons to anyone else.

He had obviously been kissing someone the other night.

Someone other than Kimi. That smear of lipstick had not appeared out of thin air.

She realized she was staring hard at Bridget's glossy red lips, and looked away, consciously relaxing her tightly curled fingers.

Suddenly, everyone around her began clapping and cheering, and Kimi hurriedly followed suit. The senior management team at the front of the room was clapping, too, and employees were pushing back their chairs, enthusiasm in their faces and their movements. Some were heading up to the front of the room where Bridget was rapidly doling out sheets of paper, while others were filing out of the training room, chattering in a half dozen languages.

"Well, this is an unexpected kettle of fish," Nigel said.

Charity, on the other side of him, gave him a deadly look. "That is *all* you have to say?"

"Well, old girl, you can win the contest just as easily as anyone else can," he quickly soothed. "But even you must admit that it's a good morale booster to involve all of the hotel staff, rather than leave the decision about the party to a small committee. You can put as many ideas into the pot as you like."

"The theme for the party has always been decided upon by the planning committee," she reminded icily.

"Sure—" Tanya leaned over Kimi and Nigel "—with a tidy little budget that you've always managed as the chair. But we're in a new hotel, Charity, with a new general manager. What's wrong with shaking things up a little?"

Charity focused her outraged and, surprisingly, hurt attention on Kimi. "Everything was fine until you came along."

"Me?" Her voice rose incredulously. "I haven't offered even one opinion about this particular debate."

Charity turned on her heel and flounced out of the training room, clearly in a huff. Nigel clucked his tongue and hurried after her, obviously fretting.

"I guess y'all don't have to care too much about the prize," Tanya said, evidently less concerned about Charity's mood than Nigel was.

Kimi gave a vague "hmm," since her complete preoccupation with the shade of Bridget's lipstick had prevented her from hearing a single detail about any prize, much less how it related to the holiday party.

"Personally, I wouldn't mind winning plane fare to the States," Tanya went on. "Then I could go back to Atlanta in April for my mother's birthday. But I'm not that creative when it comes to party themes. And to give Charity her due, she's usually top notch."

"Then her idea could well be chosen. Or is it an actual drawing of chance?"

"Not just chance. We could end up with some horrible theme. No. Senior management will select the winner after reviewing all the entries this week." She did not seem to wonder why Kimi missed the details.

"Then Charity should just move her winter wonderland idea to a more suitable space in case it snows." Though, judging from the flock of employees busily scribbling on their papers and handing them in to Bridget, Charity might have some competition.

"I doubt she'll want to. The employee party is the night before the Nguyen wedding, and the only space Charity would likely consider is the grand ballroom. She'd hate being relegated to the exhibition hall downstairs."

"Ah." Kimi knew quite well that the ballroom in question was being set and decorated the day before the wedding. That's what happened when a wedding reception became more of a theatrical production than a simple party. "That seems a shame, though. The party is obviously important to her."

"She'll get over it. She's just miffed because the decision making has been taken out of her hands."

"What about you? You should submit at least one idea," Kimi encouraged.

"I'm good at carrying out the plans that others make," Tanya said, hesitating.

"Don't sell yourself short." She could see the way Tanya's gaze sidled toward the front of the room. "What is the harm? At least think about it."

"I don't know." Tanya made a face. "Look at everyone who's giving Bridget an idea. There's nothing original about a costume party."

"Fine. But it could be *your* costume theme they go for." She yanked a piece of paper out of the portfolio pad that she had learned never to be without and quickly scribbled Tanya's name at the top. "Anything else you want to add?"

Tanya huffed, looking amused. "I don't know. Something like the movie *Casablanca*, maybe. Black-and-white and from the forties."

"Perfect." Kimi wrote it down, folded the sheet in half and held it toward Tanya.

"I'll turn the idea in if you'll turn one in."

"I have no need for the tickets," Kimi demurred.

"So?" Tanya waved her folded sheet. "It's just good fun, anyway. What's the harm," she returned pointedly.

Kimi grimaced and scrawled the first thing she could think of on another sheet. Before she could back out, Tanya snatched it and took it to the front of the room. Moments later, she returned and headed out of the room. "Come on," she told Kimi. "A bunch of us are meeting up at Seven for happy hour. You can get us comped."

"I cannot comp anyone anything," Kimi protested, but she was so surprised at the invitation that she followed along despite the homework that waited for her attention.

Even if she did foot the bill, which was the norm whenever she had socialized in the past, it was better than sitting around alone tormenting herself with images of Greg's mouth plastered over his secretary's glossy red lips.

She would have plenty of time doing that later when she was alone in her room, looking anywhere but at the connecting door to Greg's room and listening for the faint sounds of him coming and going.

When they made their way up to Seven, the holiday bedecked lounge was already crowded. Tanya grabbed Kimi's hand and pulled her through the throng until they reached a circular banquette crowded with staffers, some of whom Kimi recognized and some whom she did not. Even Charity was there, looking cozy with a man that Kimi vaguely recognized from Security. Tanya tossed out introductions as she nudged over a young man enough so that she and Kimi could sit, too. "Y'all have a head start on us," she observed, looking at the collection of cocktail glasses already littering the hammered copper table. She lifted her hand, waving over one of the cocktail waitresses and soon, Tanya's rum and coke and Kimi's cosmopolitan were added to the confusion.

The music from the live band perched on a small stage next to the dance floor was unabashedly rock and roll, and before long, the alcohol and the warmth from the crush of bodies had Kimi pulling off her suit jacket and tossing it atop those that had already been discarded by the others.

Someone ordered up sushi, more drinks were delivered and the music just got louder.

And then came the dancing.

And more drinks.

And more people crowding into Seven.

Kimi's feet were practically numb inside her Jimmy Choos from whirling around the dance floor with anyone and everyone before she called a laughing time-out and found her way back to the table to take a breather. Her martini glass had once again been replaced by a filled one. She could not quite recall how many that made.

She picked it up and sipped, looking around for the cocktail waitress. What she really wanted was a tall bottle of water and a gigantic hamburger.

Then she spotted Greg on the dance floor with Bridget and realized that the only thing she wanted, needed, was to escape.

Would he have red lipstick smeared over his lips again tonight?

She turned away from the sight.

Shin Endo stood behind her. She started with surprise and barely kept from spilling the vodka and cranberry juice concoction down the front of her thin turtleneck.

He had to lean closer and speak loudly to even be heard over the loud music. "Having fun?"

She had been until she had spotted Greg with Bridget. She lifted her glass and took another small sip, buying time until her tight throat released. "Seven is quite a place."

Shin's expression was inscrutable, though behind the severely tailored goatee he wore, his lips seemed to smile slightly. "We like to think so. Would you like to dance?"

She looked back at the dance floor, pretending that she was just checking the crowd, rather than the location of Greg and his beautiful assistant. "Why not?"

She quickly lifted her glass to her lips and drank deeply before setting it on the table and worked her way back onto the floor. Shin was a good dancer, and she knew she was making a miserable partner given the way she kept glancing behind him to Greg.

Whether fortunately or unfortunately, however, soon after she and Shin had begun, the band wrapped up with a resounding flourish, announced that they were taking a break, and before the crowded dance floor could empty, a slow ballad throbbed through the state-of-the-art sound system.

Shin deftly swept her into his arms, and continued dancing and despite herself, Kimi grinned. "Nice moves, Mr. Endo."

"I dated a dance instructor," he admitted. "She taught me a few moves."

She lifted her eyebrows humorously. "I am sure she did."

His teeth flashed and he twirled her through the slightly thinning crowd. She laughed, unexpectedly delighted.

"Mind if I cut in?"

The laughter caught in Kimi's throat. Greg stood behind Shin, his hand on the security director's shoulder.

"Can't very well say no to the boss," Shin said good-naturedly. "Thank you for the spin." He bowed to Kimi and released her to Greg.

Because she could not stop herself, Kimi's gaze slid down Greg's body and back up again. Unlike nearly everyone else in the lounge that had shed jackets and ties and name badges, he still looked wholly on duty. She knew she could either invite attention by standing like a stump in the middle of the swaying dancers, or she could move into his waiting arms and dance slowly. Against him.

Telling her heart to settle down did little good, and she put her hand in his. He took her other and situated it on his shoulder as if he recognized her hesitation and turned her smoothly again into the swaying couples.

She lifted her chin slightly, and tried to pretend that every nerve inside her had not gone into free fall. "So tomorrow is the big day. I do not suppose you are the least nervous."

He leaned over her, close enough that she could feel the warmth of his cheek against hers as he spoke close to her ear. "I can't hear you over the music."

She felt buffeted by the shiver that danced down her spine. She tilted back her head to repeat what she had said, only to find the words drying in her throat when her lips brushed against his jaw.

Accidentally?

She could not even be certain of her own actions. All she knew was that her lips were tingling from that glancing brush with the faint shadow blurring his jaw. "I...I said—" Someone bumped her from behind, jostling her closer to him. "Sorry."

"My fault." He revolved around so that his back was to the bulk of the crowd. His thumb seemed to drag slowly across her knuckles and Kimi's knees threatened to turn to water.

He leaned closer again. "Don't look at me like that." His voice sounded as raspy as his jaw had felt against her lips.

Despite the alcohol swimming so freely through her veins, she knew she was treading much more dangerous waters. She stepped closer into him, stretching up to his ear. "I cannot help it," she admitted. "What did you ask me to dance for?"

"To stop Shin from making a spectacle of himself with you."

She sucked in a stinging breath. "Mr. Endo was merely dancing," she defended and managed to plant her very sharp heel into his shoe.

He gave a muffled oath and his hold on her tightened warningly.

She smiled innocently. "Pardon my clumsiness."

"There is nothing clumsy about you," he countered.

"And you do not worry about making a spectacle with anyone?"

She could feel the warmth of his breath as his lips brushed even closer against her ear. "Do you want to hear that I was jealous?"

She pulled back to look into his face, searching his eyes for some answer that might end the confusing tangle of emotion inside her. "Were you?"

The song ended, and her words sounded suddenly loud in that breath of a moment before the strains of the next fast number geared up.

Flushing, Kimi took the escape. "Thank you—" she pulled her hand away from his and turned half away "—for the dance." She quickly left the dance floor, grabbed up her jacket and headed out, stopping only long enough to tell the hostess to charge the bill for the table to her.

She did not look back to see if Greg would follow.

Because she knew he would not.

Feeling decidedly defiant, she eschewed the service elevator and used the main bank to reach her floor.

In her room, the first thing she did was kick off her high heels and yank open a packet of coffee to start the coffeemaker. Unfortunately, her hands were trembling so badly she scattered as many grounds across the counter as she managed to pour into the filter. She swept the mess into the trash and hit the start button on the machine.

The second thing she did was sprawl facedown on the foot of her bed and groan. How often was she going to make a fool of herself where Greg was concerned?

She turned her head, eyeing the desk where her laptop and textbooks vied for space among the piles of clothing that her closets and drawers did not have room for.

If she had just stayed in school, she would not now be here in Kyoto, fighting an impossible attraction to an equally impossible man.

Would she have been better off?

She closed her eyes and looked away from her computer. The coffeemaker's soft hiss and gurgle were the only sounds in the room. But Kimi sat bolt upright when she heard a short knock on the connecting door.

"Open up, Kimi," Greg's voice was muffled and low but still distinct.

She pressed her hand against her heart and slowly slid off the bed. "Why?" She hurriedly folded down her laptop and tossed her discarded jacket over the textbooks.

"Do you want me to get a pass key?"

She fumbled with the lock and slowly opened her side of the connecting doorway. "You would not do that. It would go against your ethics."

He looked grim. "Don't be too sure. I seem willing to do all sorts of things when it comes to you."

Her hand tightened reflexively against the doorknob and

she rested her head against the solid door. "Like interrupt a perfectly innocent dance?"

"Like open this bloody damn door between us," he returned evenly. His gaze flicked from her to the door that she was using more or less as a shield. "Are you hiding someone in there?"

"Yes." The lump in her throat made it hard to speak. "The entire maintenance crew, if you must know. We are going to have an orgy. Would you like to join us?"

His lips twisted. "You've had too much to drink."

"Whereas I suppose *you* have never overindulged." Tired of keeping up the front, she turned away and padded over to her coffeemaker. She yanked out the small pot and shakily filled one of the provided porcelain cups.

She was painfully aware of him coming up behind her, but resolutely kept from lifting her gaze to the mirror on the wall above the counter and set the cup on the matching saucer. She lifted it slightly to the side. "There is enough for two cups if you want. The Taka provides the very best in amenities, even for the lowly emp—" She broke off when his hands closed over her shoulders. The coffee cup rattled in the saucer, and she hastily set it on the counter. "What do you want from me, Greg? Other than for me to go away altogether?" She finally looked up at the mirror and felt pinned in place when his gaze trapped hers there.

His thumbs roved slowly, lightly, over the point of her shoulders left bare by her sleeveless turtleneck. That was distracting enough. But the torn expression on his face was what really sent her emotions spiraling.

"You would rather that I was not here at all," she said huskily.

His lips were tight, but his touch on her shoulders was impossibly gentle. "I would rather that looking at you didn't turn my guts inside out. I would rather that I could still think straight when you walk into the room."

"Nothing distracts you from business," she whispered. "Everyone in the hotel says so."

"Nothing ever has—except you."

Why did hearing what she desperately wanted to hear make her also want to cry? She swallowed hard and managed to pull her gaze free, staring hard instead at absolutely nothing to keep the burning behind her eyes from becoming anything more. "I didn't come here to be a distraction to anyone."

"Some things don't happen by choice. You can't help being distracting any more than the sun can help rising in the morning."

"That doesn't sound like a compliment coming in such a terse tone." She carefully centered the coffee cup and saucer in front of the coffeemaker. "If you do not believe it is choice that brought you into my room, then you should go. I know there are many things that we cannot choose in life, and maybe who we are at—" she curled her fingers against her palms "—attracted to, is one of those things. But what we do about it *is* a choice."

"A damned costly one." His voice was low. "I was jealous. I didn't like seeing you dancing with Shin."

"It was merely a dance between coworkers. It was not like you and your...your assistant."

His head jerked back. "Bridget? What the hell is that supposed to mean?"

It was too late to back down now. Kimi turned to face him, pressing her hands against the counter behind her. "She is the one, is she not? The other woman you were kissing?"

Chapter Nine

Greg stared at Kimi, trying to decipher the coils inside her mind. "No, I was *not* kissing Bridget. She's my secretary for God's sake. Where on earth did you get that ridiculous idea?"

"She is very beautiful."

"Sure. And so is Grace Ishida and about three dozen other women I could name off the top of my head who work for me. I'm not sleeping with them, either."

Her shoulder lifted diffidently. "I heard otherwise."

He let out an impatient snort. "Gossip. What did I tell you about gossip in hotels? There *never* has to be any basis to it. It just grows all on its own."

Her long lashes veiled her eyes. "Then who was it? The one who you would be smarter to be with?"

"An attorney I know. Nobody who matters." He lifted her chin until she had to look at him. "I do not sleep with my employees."

"Not even in your other hotels?"

"Not even there," he assured flatly.

"Then why do you choose to come into my room now? You said we should stay away from each other. And I have done so!"

He needed no reminder that he was the one who kept crossing his own uncrossable line. He reached into his pocket and pulled out a plastic wrapped employee name badge. "Here." The badge was nothing more than an excuse, though.

He could lie to everyone on the planet about his reasons, but he couldn't lie to himself. Not anymore.

He'd wanted to see her.

End of story.

She slowly took the badge and peeled off the clinging protective wrap. Then she smoothed her fingertip across the brushed brass surface engraved with her name.

He shoved his hands in his pockets and paced toward the window. "The first one that came back said Kimiko. I thought you'd prefer it to say Kimi. That's why it took this long to get it. I had Human Resources reorder another."

"Hai." Her voice was nearly inaudible. "I do prefer Kimi. Thank you."

"What's wrong with Kimiko, anyway?"

She slipped off the magnetic bar on the back of the badge and turned to face the mirror again, positioning the badge over the sweater that lovingly clung to her willowy curves. "I just prefer Kimi. It sounds less—it sounds more…Western. More approachable." He caught the grimace she made in the mirror before she turned back to look at him, the name badge in place. "How does it look?"

As effective as armor.

Or it should have been.

He walked behind her desk. Another layer between them. Knowing he was a damn pathetic excuse of a manager if he couldn't keep his hands to himself.

"It's just a badge," he said, whether in response to her question or the impossible debate inside him, he didn't know.

Her lips curved sadly. "It is my first employee badge. And if I fail here at this hotel, I fear that my father will never allow me to wear another badge bearing a Taka logo."

He knew how much his career mattered to him. He was just beginning to appreciate how much the job might truly mean to her.

He eyed the laptop nearly obscured by the mound of clothing on her desk. "Grace tells me you have the Nguyens' wedding coordinator eating out of your hand."

She pressed her lips together for a moment. "Mr. Tessier is not so bad."

Greg had heard plenty of complaints otherwise before Kimi had come on the scene. "She also says that you are doing an excellent job in general."

"I will remind her of that when she fills out my three-month review."

"She won't need to be reminded," he assured. Grace had been receptive to the idea of Kimi working there all along.

It was only Greg who'd had an issue with it.

He moved a pair of shoes from the upholstered desk chair and sat. Kimi had him feeling like a teenaged kid who'd just discovered the wonders of women. She also had him feeling every one of his thirty-two years, and then some.

He pulled at his constricting tie. "You needed to stay in the Mahogany for the closet space alone."

She gave him a faint smile, but stayed near the coffeemaker. "I was able to dispose of my excess luggage, but I confess that I do not find it so easy to part with much of my clothing. I kept picturing my friend Lana's face whenever I added something to my giveaway pile. She wants to be a fashion designer."

He picked up the top item on one of the folded stacks on the desk and shook the diminutive item out.

Tasty. The memorable stitching came into view.

"That was one of hers," Kimi murmured. She shook her head, looking regretful. "I should have taken time to change on the flight over that first day. You had every right to disapprove."

He set the patch of fabric that passed for a skirt back on the pile. What he'd been was overbearing and damned intent on establishing his authority.

"I probably could have been more tactful," he admitted.

"Probably?"

He grimaced and silence, thick and pulsing, settled between them until finally, Kimi cleared her throat and moved, only to perch herself gingerly on the very corner of her bed. "Who would have thought we would come to these admissions?"

"Why is being more Western important to you?"

She shot him a startled look. "Excuse me?"

"You said you liked going by Kimi because it sounded more Western."

She brushed her hands down her thighs and rose from the bed. "It is merely a nickname. You don't go by Gregory, yet that is *your* name."

"Americans are always in a hurry. We shorten everything."

"Then my U.S. citizenship is not misplaced," she said promptly. "Kimi is shorter than Kimiko. Do not make more of my preference than it is. I told you I missed nothing about Japan when I left."

"But you chose to come here."

"I asked for a job, and this is where I was sent."

"Do you want to leave?"

"You would like that, would you not?"

He exhaled. Not as much as he should. What he ought do was leave her room. Go back through the connecting doorway, close it, lock it and throw away the key.

Instead, he picked up one of the small framed photographs perched on the ledge of the window that overlooked nothing. A teenaged Kimi, her father and stepmother dressed in scuba gear smiled back at the camera, looking carefree. "How old were you when this was taken?"

"Fifteen." She stopped next to him and took the frame in her hands, looking at it. "We were in the Caribbean for a vacation. Have you ever been there?"

When he was fifteen, he and his mother had been living in a single-wide trailer parked behind the convenience store where he worked. "Yeah. I did a stint in the Caymans at an all-inclusive resort when I was a few years older than you are now." Two months of sand and sun and thinking that he'd fallen for a wealthy young jet-setter named Sydney who was staying there.

"I think you may have traveled more than I have." Kimi's voice pulled him back from the memory that no longer held any sting, but still served as a reminder that some lines aren't meant to be crossed. Not permanently.

"Not in the same way," he assured dryly.

She leaned past him to replace the frame with the others and he had to fist his hands to keep them from breaching the paltry few inches between them.

But instead of straightening again and moving safely away, she seemed to freeze. Then she slowly lifted her long lashes, casting him a hesitant, sidelong look. "Even my father learned that mixing business with pleasure was not always a terrible thing. Sometimes it is the most successful in all ways."

"When your father married your stepmother, she was a wealthy woman at the helm of a significant American media company. I'm pretty sure he'd feel differently if he knew that any of that kind of mixing involved his daughter and someone on his payroll."

Her voice went even softer. "He does not need to know everything."

Could the room be any hotter? He yanked his tie another inch looser. "Is there anything in your life you do that your father *doesn't* find out about?"

Her lashes fell again. "There are a few," she said after a moment. She looked up at him again, but her gaze didn't seem to make it any higher than his mouth.

"Like what?"

"You wish to have proof?" She leaned past him suddenly and pushed a pile of clothing off the desk. She picked up the thick textbook she revealed. "Will this suffice? He does not know I am finishing my degree."

"Why not?"

"Because I am as contrary as everyone says."

He took the textbook from her. "This is what you've been doing every night. The reasons you raid the kitchen at two in the morning."

"I am sorry to disillusion you about my partying ways." She snatched the book and pitched it after the clothing and impetuously fastened her mouth to his.

He'd been around too long not to know that lightning could strike twice. That the one kiss they'd shared wasn't just some random fluke.

Kissing Kimi Taka—no matter how many times—was like lassoing lightning. Intoxicating, exhilarating and dangerous as hell.

Even knowing that, it took him too damn long to tear his mouth from hers and when he did, he found his hands were wrapped around those long, silky skeins of dark hair. "Dammit to *hell.*"

She pressed her lips together as if savoring the taste of him. Her voice was husky when she finally spoke. *"Sumimasen."*

He let out a strangled groan. "You're not sorry."

She sucked in an audible breath. "No. I am not sorry." Her fingers fluttered over the loosened knot of his tie. "Does it help if I take all responsibility? I kissed you. It is not as if you were an interested participant. And we can blame my forwardness on the cosmopolitans I had earlier."

His gaze fastened on her face, seeing past the bravado to the uncertainty that had a much more effective way of sneaking inside and grabbing him by the gut. "If you think I'm not interested, you haven't been paying attention very well."

"Interested but unwilling."

"Kimi—"

"I am not in the habit of begging for a man's attention."

"Because most any man would fall over themselves for you. Which you well know."

"But not you." She pressed her lips together for a moment and her lashes swept down again. "This would be the time for you to say that my interest is only heightened because of your resistance. That I only want what I cannot get. Contrary, remember?"

She was definitely a woman of contradictions. "There's no possible way this can end well."

"This?"

His hands clamped around her hips and he pulled her down onto his lap. *"This."* His voice was tight.

Her eyes widened and color bloomed on her cheeks. She couldn't fail to miss his meaning. Not when "this" was a plainly obvious presence there between them.

"I do not wish to think about endings."

"Honey, there's always an ending."

"And there is the *now*," she countered. "Do you not know the importance of living in the moment?" She slid her hands beneath the lapels of his jacket and they seemed to burn right through his shirt to his chest. "You run a hotel that seduces its clientele into that very luxurious thing."

He was the one feeling seduced and it wasn't a particularly accustomed sensation. "Those are the clients," he corrected. "I'm not one of them."

"Do you not wish to be like that, though?" She leaned into him, managing to fit her curves even more fully against him. She fiddled with his tie. "Just once in a while, to be just a man, and not always the boss?"

"I am the boss. Your boss."

She managed to slide the tie free and let it dangle it from her fingertips. "And if you were not?"

He grimaced. "Yes, well, I won't be if your parents fire me."

"That is not what I meant."

He grabbed the tie. "You do plan on going somewhere, then? I thought you weren't a quitter. Isn't that what you've been trying to convince me of these past few weeks?"

"If I go elsewhere," she pressed.

"But you work here."

"If I did *not*?"

He let out a short breath. "I don't know why I should be surprised when that persistent streak of yours makes its way to the surface."

"Energy and persistence conquer all things."

He let out a short breath. "Quoting Benjamin Franklin ought to douse the problem we've got between us, but it doesn't."

She slid her hand behind his neck, feathering her fingertips through his hair. "It does not feel like it is a problem that is between us." Bright color bloomed in her cheeks. But that didn't stop her slender hips from rocking almost undetectably against him.

But he still felt her. Still wanted more of her.

He caught her fingers when they slid down his neck again to seek the button holding his strangling collar closed. "It's a problem because you're Kimi Taka." He knew he sounded like a broken record, but there it was.

"Could we not just forget who my family is? Just…for a while?"

He let go of her hand and slid his palms along the impossibly fine line of her jaw, cupping her face. "You don't understand how often I do forget." He brushed his thumb slowly over her lower lip. "But the fact remains, Kimi, that you and I are in two different worlds. I'm the mutt—"

She huffed, rolling her eyes. "Please."

"—who's managed to work his way up in the world," he continued doggedly. "But that doesn't mean I'm ever really a part of that world."

"You are a snob," she accused huskily.

"I'm a realist."

"That sounds worse."

He could feel the butterfly beat of her pulse throbbing against her satin smooth throat. "You are Mahogany Suite material, Kimi. That's where you belong. Even if you don't want to remember that today, sooner or later you will and you'll leave me in the dust without a second glance."

"You are wrong, you know." She didn't look away from him despite the sudden glisten in her eyes.

"Like it or not, I've got a few more years under my belt to have learned some about human nature. If things were different—" His voice was low. Nearly hoarse.

"That is an easy thing to say, is it not? Because I will always be who I am. And you will always hold it against me, so we will never know."

"I don't hold it against you."

"Are you certain? If I were anyone else, I believe you would not hold back." She pressed herself even more boldly against him, and the soft catch of her breath when she did so nearly undid him. He could feel every breath she drew as if he breathed them for himself.

His hands found their way back into her hair. "You're killing me here," he muttered.

The color in her cheeks deepened. Her eyes were dark and nakedly vulnerable. "I would rather share a different little death with you."

He tucked her brow against his, bracing against the blast of heat plowing through him. "*That* kind of little death is likely to blow the roof off the Taka."

"Well—" Kimi twisted her head around until her lips hovered against his. Her own boldness shocked her. "*This* Taka, at least."

She gasped when Greg abruptly rose from the desk chair, lifting her along with him, only to toss her across her bed. The pillows at the head bounced, one slid off onto the floor.

She stared up at him, her heart racing. "Greg?"

He followed her down, catching her wrists in his hands and looming over her. "You sure about this, Kimi? Do you want just mind-blowing sex?" His hooded gaze seemed to burn over her face, setting off a clenching wave of heat that spread through her body. He slowly lowered his head until his lips grazed tantalizingly over her earlobe. "That's something I can deliver."

He had her trapped in such a miasma of desire, she could not doubt that particular talent of his. Her fingers curled, instinctively wanting to touch him, but he still held her wrists captive.

"Or are you going to want more?"

Her head pressed back into the soft bedding. If there were more, she was uncertain she could survive, and the only place he was touching her—other than that maddening non-kiss— was her wrists. "M-more?"

He finally lifted his head, and she managed to drag in a shuddering breath. His jaw looked carved from stone. "You won't get more from me," he warned. "Gossip around this place can spring up from nothing but it just as easily broadcasts the facts. Haven't you paid attention? I don't do relationships. The only thing I care about is my career."

"You care about a lot more than that." Her voice shook. "A person only has to see the way you work to know that. You surround yourself with *people* you care about. Mr. Endo and Grace and Lyle."

"I hired them because they are the best at what they do."

"I believe you brought them here, away from the various places they had been working because they are like family to you," she countered swiftly.

"The only family I have is my mother, and I would no more want her working anywhere near me than I'd want to stick my head in a noose. Which is exactly where your father will want my head if he gets word that I'm sleeping with his daughter."

Her nerves felt ready to jump out of her skin. Her legs moved restlessly. She had to swallow hard. "*Are* you? Sleeping with his daughter?"

His eyes stared into hers for what seemed an eternity. "Every time I close my eyes." His hold gentled, no longer shackling her wrists, and she couldn't restrain the faint moan that rose in her throat when his palms flattened against hers, his long fingers sliding between hers. "Everything about this is wrong, and I know it, and I still can't make myself stop wanting you."

"Stop trying," she whispered. She tightened her fingers against his hands, levering herself up to meet his mouth. "*Dozo.*" She breathed against him. "Please."

He groaned, and swept her against him, his hands slipping down her spine, cradling her over him as he turned against the mattress, pulling her hips tight against his.

He swallowed the cry she could not contain, and then his hands were pushing beneath her thin sweater, dragging it upward, his warm palms sweeping up her spine, sending shudders dancing through her limbs. When he could draw the sweater no higher, she sat up, only to have to steady herself with a hand on his hard abdomen when she felt the full extent of his arousal against her.

His gaze was intent. "This is the time to stop, Kimi."

She drew her knees alongside his strong hips, saw the effect that had in the way his jaw tightened and his green gaze sharpened. "I don't think so," she said huskily, and tugged the sweater over her head and tossed it aside. His gaze dropped to her breasts and she felt her skin tighten as if he had touched her. She slowly undid the back clasp of her sheer black bra. "Stopping now is the last thing I want."

"And the first?"

She slid the straps off her shoulders and let the bra fall away. Evasion was simply beyond her. "I want you to touch me." Her breasts were so full and tight, they ached.

His fingers flexed against her hips. "Where?" His voice seemed to come from somewhere deep inside him.

She stared at him. This man who so confounded her thoughts, her body, her heart.

She pressed her fingertips to her lips. "Here." She let her fingertips drift down her throat until they reached her breasts. She slowly covered them, her hands shaking. "Here."

She saw, as well as heard, the sharp breath he drew in through his nose.

Emboldened, she trailed her fingers down the valley between her breasts until she reached the waist of her silk slacks. "Here."

He suddenly jackknifed upward, catching her mouth with his, kissing her so deeply she felt faint. Or maybe that was his hands, covering her breasts, grazing her flesh, tormenting her nipples into even more frenzied peaks. Then she felt his knuckles brush her abdomen, as he freed the clasp of her slacks and drew down the zipper. "Where else?"

Fire ripped along her nerves, but shyness tore alongside it. "Greg. Wait. I—" She ducked her chin, suddenly aware of how bare she was, and how clothed he remained.

He drew his hands away only to tilt up her chin. His expression softened. "What is it, Kimi?"

She knew she should tell him. Tell him now, before it was too late, that she was a virgin. "I...not *what*," she said weakly. *"Where."* She suddenly pulled at his shirt, tugging it from his trousers. "Touch me everywhere," she breathed. "But I want to touch you, too." Her hands finally met warm flesh. She felt his muscles bunch beneath her fingertips as she tossed aside the shirt. And she felt even dizzier as her hands slowly drifted up his torso.

Muscle. A whorl of soft hair that felt oddly crisp against her palms as they spread over the widening breadth of his chest. The heavy thud of his heart when her hand paused over it.

"You are so beautiful." The words came without thought. He truly was, in the most masculine of ways.

He, of course, snorted softly. "That's my line." He kissed the tip of her shoulder. The curve of her neck where her pulse sped frantically against the flicker of his tongue. His head dipped even farther, and she felt his kiss slide downward, over one breast, then the other, closer and closer until she felt his breath brush over her nipple.

Her head fell back, her eyes closing. "There," she gasped, and cried out when his mouth finally covered one tormented peak. Pleasure careened through her, aiming straight for the very center of her. She felt herself falling, heard the keening moan coming from her that she could not seem to stop.

And she could only grab for him as her world tipped on its axis.

She was barely conscious of the way he groaned her name, the way he stripped the rest of their clothing away and hauled her toward the center of the bed. Then he was leaning over her, threading his hand through her hair, spreading it wide, as his mouth found hers again. "I want you to do that again with me inside you." His low words vibrated intoxicatingly against her lips.

"Yes." She could not seem to form another word to save her soul. Her hands weakly closed over his broad shoulders. "Yes."

His kiss swallowed the word as he settled against her and at last she felt him *there*. No clothing between them. No barriers.

Just the two of them.

She shifted, lifting herself against him, gripped with sudden impatience. All she wanted was more. More of him. More of them. More of that undying pleasure flooding her cells, and the only thing that would satisfy was *him*.

He let out a low growl and ran his hands along her thighs, and sank deeply.

Heat, pressure, pleasure, it all screamed through her at once.

But she could not stop the sharp gasp at the unfamiliar invasion, no matter how badly she wanted.

He went utterly still against her, an oath on his lips. "What the—"

"Stay." She breathed hard, pressing her mouth against the hard bulge of his shoulder. The pain was already passing, far outshadowed by the spiraling pleasure, and she twined her arms around his back.

Yet he still managed to lift himself above her. "You're a virgin."

She moistened her lips. If she had expected anger, she would have been wrong, for it was shock…and pain…that tightened his face.

"I wanted to tell you." She could still feel him, insistent and full inside her and instinctively rocked against him, nearly moaning again at the intoxicating sensations. "I did. But it does not matter."

His teeth bared and he caught her hips in his hard hands, whether to stop her motion or to encourage, she couldn't tell. "Doesn't *matter*?"

She slid her legs against his. Ran her hands down his spine. Pulled herself even more tightly into his broad, tall body. "Not anymore." She rocked against him and had to press her mouth against his shoulder to muffle her moan of pleasure.

His fingers dug into her hips, as if to push her away again, but with an oath, instead he drove deeper.

Again. And again, sending a wildfire streaking through her that eclipsed everything that had gone before. She was only vaguely aware of his name on her lips as the coil inside her tightened until she thought she might scream from it, and then his hands slid against hers, fingers tightening, and he murmured her name in a low breath as he tensed, and just like that she slid off the precipice with him, exploding in ecstasy.

His head fell to her breast, great breaths racking through his broad shoulders. Her head fell back weakly against the bare mattress—somehow they had managed to tear the sheets halfway off of it. "As an American, you are not *always* in a hurry," she managed to say breathlessly.

"Damn it, Kimi!" He yanked away from her and pushed off the bed, leaving her gasping. Without a seeming shred of modesty for his nudity, he stood at the side of the bed and glared at her. "Is this a joke to you?"

She pushed herself up on her arms. "Of course not."

"Then you should have told me."

"So that you could think me even more of a child?"

"I might have thought you were more mature for admitting the truth!"

She winced. "We will never know. My virginity is—was—mine to give as I chose."

"Yeah, well, if it didn't matter as you say, then why the hell didn't you get rid of it with one of those guys you were always with in the gossip rags?"

She realized she was staring at him and couldn't seem to make herself stop. She had to fist her hands in the downy comforter to keep from reaching out and closing her fingers around him. "Would you have really preferred that?"

He raked his hands through his hair, leaving the short strands standing in spikes. "No." His answer was brutal and short.

She moistened her lips and swallowed the knot in her throat. Her body shamelessly wanted him all over again.

She feared her heart was on the verge of endlessly needing him.

She released the comforter and lifted her hand, palm upward. "Then come back to me, Greg."

His jaw canted. "What if I've gotten you pregnant?"

A sweet pang speared her. What if he had? The thought should horrify her, but it did not. "I have been on the pill for several years," she told him truthfully.

His eyebrow lifted, sardonic.

"To regulate my cycle," she finished, squelching the defensiveness that rose inside her. "As you have discovered, there was not much other reason. Believe it or not, it is a fairly common practice."

"Imagine my relief."

She lifted her chin. "There is no need to be sarcastic."

"No. Of course not. I just stole the virginity of the child of the very two people who entrusted her well-being to me!"

She scrambled off the bed, tossing her tumbled hair out of her eyes and behind her shoulders, and stood in front of him. "First of all, I am not a child. Secondly, I came here to work, not to be babysat by *you*. And most important, get it through your head, Greg, that one cannot steal what is freely given!"

His hands closed around her and he hauled her off her toes, right up to his nose. "Why now, Kimi? Why me?"

Her lips parted. "Because I—" She broke off before she humiliated herself even more and wriggled until he released her.

She could not possibly love this man who had so little use for her.

Could she?

"Why not you," she asked flippantly. "Why not now? If I am banished here to Kyoto, at least I managed to get some practical use out of it!" Before he could see the tears burning in her eyes, she knelt down and snatched up his shirt, yanking it over her shoulders. Her fingers were trembling too badly to bother with buttons, and she just clutched it together at her waist as she strode over to the open doorway connecting their rooms. "But now that it is done, you might as well go."

"Dismissing the help, are you, Kimiko?"

She lifted her chin, avoiding his gaze. "You will think what you want no matter what I say."

He did not bother collecting the remainder of his clothing. Not his trousers nor even his shoes.

He strode through the doorway.

She could not be certain which side closed first.

Hers.

Or his.

But close they did and, once they were, Kimi turned away from the sight. She could not even bury her face in her pillows or in her tumbled bed. Not when, despite everything, her body was still yearning for his.

Chapter Ten

"Good afternoon. Welcome to the Taka Kyoto."

From her position behind the reception desk where Kimi had been hurriedly training with Sue to help fill in for a regular who had been stricken with the flu, she watched Greg greet the guests milling around the lobby.

For some reason she had expected the second week after their opening to be much slower than it had been during the first week.

Today, however, the bellmen were still in constant demand, couriering carts of luggage across the marble and wood floors. Michel St. Jacques, the concierge, had yet another small but steady line of guests awaiting his special attention. As they had since they had opened to guests, four young, pretty women whom Kimi remembered from the banquet crew were rotating through the lobby, offering trays of delectable hors d'oeuvres and drinks. The water in the fountain offered a soft, rippling backdrop to the trio of musicians stationed nearby, playing familiar holiday carols.

There was a calmly organized flow to everything, but Kimi could still feel the heightened energy that hovered beneath. She wished she could have felt a little of that energy herself, but nothing seemed able to displace the disquiet that had filled her since her and Greg's lovemaking had ended in such failure.

None of which showed on her face, she felt certain, as she slid two newly programmed key cards into a jacket and handed them across to the couple she had just checked in to the hotel. "We hope you enjoy your stay with us, Mr. and Mrs. Peterson."

"It's our thirtieth anniversary," Mrs. Peterson admitted in a hushed tone. "My husband surprised me with a world tour."

From the corner of her eye, she saw Ambassador Diggins and his wife cross the lobby from the elevators and latch on to Greg.

Kimi realized she was watching him too hungrily and quickly turned her focus back on the Petersons. "That's very romantic. Congratulations." Kimi made a note in the registration file about the anniversary. She did not know the procedure, but she knew there was some sort of special amenity the hotel would provide to honor the occasion.

"Honey, come see the garden." Mr. Peterson was wandering toward the fountain and the expansive windows beyond. "It's just beginning to snow."

"The gardens are all beautiful here," Kimi encouraged. "Joon will take care of your luggage. It will be waiting for you in your room if you would like to explore first." The bellman was at the ready as soon as she gave him a glance.

Mrs. Peterson smiled and hurried after her husband, tucking her arm in his.

Kimi watched them go. Thirty years. She held back a sigh and waited until Sue finished with her guest before asking her what they could do for the Peterson's anniversary. She had just started ordering the gift basket Sue recommended to be sent to the couple's room when Tanya appeared.

"Mail room delivered this for you this morning." Tanya

handed over a padded envelope. "Thought it might be important since it came express from the States."

"Thanks." She tore open the envelope and glanced inside, though she knew what it would contain simply from the shipping label.

Her college diploma.

Considering everything, she ought to feel more elated with the delivery. Her gaze lifted, easily tracking Greg. He stood near the elevators now, along with the ambassador and his wife. A moment later, the couple disappeared from view.

Kimi closed the envelope and slid it beneath the counter, out of sight.

"Charity called in with the flu," Tanya was saying in a confiding whisper. "Whether she's really sick or just using the excuse to avoid the staff party tonight is debatable."

"I'm sorry it was not your movie theme that was selected."

"I never figured it would be," Tanya said easily. "I think your poolside Monte Carlo night will be a lot of fun, but I don't know what the big secret about it is. You could have put your name on the submission. Or at least admitted that it was your idea when they selected it."

Kimi shrugged. "I would not wish anyone to believe there was favoritism involved." Truthfully, she had been stunned when the announcement had been made about the selection. It was just another irony in her world, these days, she supposed.

"Right. 'Cause it's not like you can't afford your own plane tickets back to the States." Tanya rolled her eyes humorously. "It's your call, though. So you think you'll be off reception soon?"

"Tomorrow for certain, what with the Nguyen wedding tomorrow evening."

Tanya grinned. "Be good to get that one off the plate, won't it? I'll see you tonight, right?"

"I would not miss it. I want to see that dress you have been talking about for a week now."

With a little wave Tanya headed back in the direction she had come, leaving Kimi to finish the Peterson's gift basket order.

But her eyes kept straying to Greg.

It had been nearly two weeks since the debacle in her room. Two weeks since they had said more than one word directly to the other.

Two weeks of pure misery.

"Well, my word, look who is playing receptionist." The familiar female voice was full of laughter, and surprised, Kimi looked over to see her stepsister, Jenny, heading toward her. Her husband, Richard, was following behind, pushing a stroller, though the intended occupant of it was currently cradled in his daddy's arms. Jenny stopped in front of the desk. The striking green eyes that were so like Helen's were sparkling. "I thought you said they'd hidden you in the basement in sales."

"I'm pinch-hitting up here." Kimi left the computer and hurried around the long reception desk and hugged Jenny. "I didn't know you were coming in today."

"Richard decided to come in a day early so he could pop over to the TAKA-Hanson office in Tokyo." She turned and took the baby from her husband when he reached them.

"Hey, kiddo." Richard swallowed her in a bear hug, nearly lifting her off her toes. "Everything's looking good here."

"I have not burned down the place," she confirmed wryly, tugging down the hem of her black jacket. "Sue can check you in. *I* want to see my nephew."

"Not even three months old and letting us know he doesn't like the long flight from Chicago," Jenny told her wryly as she passed over the baby.

Kimi cradled her nephew up to her nose. "What are they saying about you, little Mr. Warren?" She kissed Jason's admittedly cranky-looking face.

He wrinkled his brow and let out a wail.

"Told you," Jenny said. "I'll take him back."

"It's all right." Kimi settled the baby against her shoulder, patting his back. "We are not so bad at this, are we," she crooned against his sweet-smelling head and carried him toward the fountain.

She stood next to it, and took Jason's tiny hand and grazed it against the sheet of falling water, dislodging the perfect, glassy surface.

Sure enough, he forgot about the big, fat tears that were rolling down his round little cheeks and wriggled his hand right back into the water.

Kimi laughed softly and pressed her lips to his bald head. "Nothing like the simple pleasures, is there?"

"Nothing like it." Greg's voice came from behind her.

She whirled around, startled.

Jason whimpered.

She stepped back again, so he could reach the waterfall and like magic, his whimpering stopped. "This is my nephew," she told Greg in a cool voice. "I will return to my duties in a moment."

His lips tightened. "I wasn't planning to chastise you for greeting your own family."

Of course not. As far as he was concerned, she and her family were on one side of the great divide while he was on the other. Fortunately, she was saved from further conversation when Jenny and Richard joined them and Greg slid seamlessly into the ultimate general manager, welcoming them with that letter-perfect graciousness that was neither ingratiating nor overbearing. It was almost a relief when Jenny started talking shop—media relations shop, that was.

"That's my cue," Richard drawled humorously. "You go take care of business, and my man and I will unpack your steamer trunks."

Jenny gave him a tsking look. "Don't exaggerate. I only brought the necessities."

Richard grinned at Greg. "To my wife, necessities usually involve half a dozen suitcases. I've learned it's a family trait."

Kimi felt Greg's gaze but didn't return it. She kissed Jason's little starfish fingers, wiping away the water, and handed him over to his father. "I had better return to the desk." There were three people waiting to be attended.

"We'll get together for dinner tonight," Jenny said.

"I can't. The staff holiday party is tonight."

Jenny's brows lifted a little, but she did not argue as she leaned over and gave Kimi another hug. "Well, we're here through the New Year, so there'll be plenty of time to catch up either before or after the rest of the clan starts descending."

Kimi smiled brightly. "That will be great." She quickly headed across to reception again and took up her temporary post at one of the computers. "Welcome to the Taka Kyoto." She greeted the guest who immediately moved over to her from Sue's line.

She did not look again across the lobby, but it did not matter since Greg and Jenny disappeared soon after Richard and the baby did, presumably to go over business matters.

She did not see Greg again for the rest of the afternoon. Carter Janes, the assistant manager he had recently hired even took over the greeting duties in the lobby and was still at it when Kimi's replacement appeared for her evening shift.

Working on her feet all day in reception was a lot more tiring than she would have expected, but Kimi still went down to the sales office to check on things there. The office was already cleared out; most of the staff was probably off getting ready for the holiday party that night. Thanks to rotating schedules in the other departments, Kimi knew that every staff member would have an opportunity to spend time at the party if they chose.

She listened to the six messages left by Anton Tessier and left her own message on his machine in return assuring him that all of his concerns had already been addressed, then went up to the ballroom one last time to see that the setup had been completed for the wedding the following day.

Everything was in place. Just as it had been when she had last checked during her lunch break.

With no more excuses to avoid doing so, she finally went to her room to change clothes for the staff party. Unfortunately, she had never felt less in the mood for a celebration. Not even one arranged to fit her hastily scrawled and anonymously suggested theme.

She flipped through the clothing in her too-full closet. Greg would certainly be at the party. He was the head of all staff, after all.

Her hand paused over a sheer slip of a dress. It was Lana's design—one that she had shoved into Kimi's stuff that last day in New York. Spaghetti straps, a deeply plunged back, the finest weave of oyster-colored silk. Kimi had not worn it yet because it practically screamed that she could wear nothing of substance beneath it, but she had not had the strength to remove it from her closet altogether when she had been culling for space.

Her jaw set, and she yanked it off the hanger and tossed it onto the bed. Then she called up to the shoe shop on the Mezzanine level, told the clerk what she was looking for and asked that they be sent to her room.

After that, she took a shower and attacked her face and her long hair with every tool she possessed.

By the time she arrived at the party, one floor up on five, it was well into full swing. Employees and their guests were clustered around the gaming tables that had been brought in and situated around the magnificent pool. Tuxedoed servers that had been hired in for the night circulated among them bearing trays of champagne flutes and hors d'oeuvres. Music thrummed through the space, and there was a crowd already formed on the dance floor that had been erected in the space ordinarily taken up by the pool lounge chairs that were now nowhere in sight.

She stopped at the check-in table where Tanya and Nigel were doling out chips and drink tickets. "Nice turnout. You two look smashing." Tanya's sequined blue gown and sparkling jewelry would have sent Lana into paroxysms of delight.

Nigel, who was surprisingly subdued and handsome in a classic black tux, was staring at her. "Who are you on the warpath for, darling?"

"It is a party." She lifted her shoulder. "I thought I should dress for the occasion, too."

Tanya laughed. "Honey, in that dress, one might think you *forgot* the dress." She handed over Kimi's allotment of chips. "Go get whoever he is, girl."

Kimi took the chips though she had no particular desire to play. The games were not for money, of course, but for prizes for the winners with the highest number of chips. Keeping an eye out for Greg, she wandered among the tables, gave away more than half of her chips to young Marco who looked charmingly uncomfortable in his white bow tie and black dinner jacket where he was miserably losing at roulette, and exchanged the champagne in her glass with sparkling water.

She had been at one of the blackjack tables for nearly an hour and had tripled the number of chips that she had given Marco when she saw Greg enter the pool area. Even though she had the advantage of seeing him before he saw her, it felt as though every cell in her body went into hyperdrive.

"Ma'am? Would you like a card?"

"Hai." She did not wait to see what the dealer dealt; nearly any card at all would put her over twenty-one.

She watched Greg cross the room to where Bridget and Grace were sitting at a table loaded with the casino prizes. Bridget handed him a pile of envelopes and he commandeered the DJ's microphone.

"Is everyone having a good time?"

A round of cheers met the question and from where she sat, she could see the tilted grin he gave. "I'm not going to stand up here and bend your ears for long—" he waited until the few hoots that earned died down "—but I do have a few items of business." He rolled his eyes at the collective boos. "No appreciation." He shook his head dolefully. "Maybe I shouldn't pass these out?" He waved the stack of envelopes that Bridget had given him and chuckled at the range of multilingual comments that elicited. "I thought so." He went on to announce various employee awards, some serious, some not. "And our last prize should be going to the person who submitted the theme for tonight's event, but whoever it was left their name off their submission."

"It was me," Marco called out at the same time as several others.

Greg laughed. "Yeah. That's what I thought. Since we ended up with some plane tickets to give away as a result, I'm going to turn things over to Grace Ishida who'll give away the tickets along with the other door prizes. Before I go, though—because we *all* know everyone has a better party if the boss isn't around to see it—" he waited out the cheering reaction "—I want to tell you that everyone has done a spectacular job with our first few weeks of operation. We wanted to make Taka Kyoto the best in its class and we are well on the way thanks to all of you."

"And thanks to *you*, Mr. Sherman." Grace took over the microphone, and Greg waved off the cheers he earned as he left the dais. True to his word, he headed more or less directly toward the pool area entrance.

"Split my chips among you," Kimi told the other three players, and quickly slid off the padded stool, deliberately setting a course to cross Greg's.

She knew the instant he spotted her because of the sliver of electricity that burrowed along her veins. That, and the fact that for a very brief moment he looked gratifyingly poleaxed.

"Good evening, Mr. Sherman. I barely recognize you without the tie." Of all the men present, he was only one of few without any sort of neckwear. Instead, he wore a thin black crewneck sweater beneath an equally black jacket. She doubted that he had chosen the uncharacteristic look because it made his light eyes stand out even more, but the effect was there nonetheless. She lifted her champagne flute, sipping her water though she could just as easily have chugged the entire contents because she felt so suddenly parched. "You throw a nice party."

His gaze burned from her face down to her toes. "Are you making some sort of statement, Ms. Taka?"

"I cannot imagine what you mean." She shook her head slightly and brushed a spiral of hair behind her shoulder.

He drew her away from the bulk of the crowd even though they were much more interested in the door prizes that Grace was giving away than listening in on their hushed exchange. "You're practically naked."

She tsked, keeping an amused expression on her face though it nearly killed her to do so. "You of all people should be able to discern the difference." It was the color and cut of the dress that was deceptive. The fabric itself was absolutely opaque.

His eyes could have spawned a typhoon they were filled with such sudden fury. "I warned you about dressing appropriately."

"But I am not on duty," she reminded smoothly. "I left my name badge in my room."

"That's hardly the point, Kimi."

She smiled humorlessly. "Then will you be issuing my marching orders now?"

"Is that what you want? For me to fire you?"

Maybe. It would certainly make things easier for her. She could go home with her tail between her legs and her family would probably not think a single thing about it.

But that was the old Kimi.

"There is no need to get yourself worked up, Mr. Sherman.

It is just a dress. I simply grabbed whatever I could reach in my tiny little closet."

"I doubt that excuse of a dress takes up much room."

She cast her eyes down, smiling demurely despite the shocking desire to drive her exquisitely pointed shoe into his shin. "Not much room at all," she agreed. "Every woman here is in dressy cocktail attire. Do you plan to chastise all of them, too?"

"Your father should have put you over his knee more often."

"Quite possibly. But it is too late for that, now." She tilted her champagne flute and drank down the rest of her sparkling water.

"Is it?" He looked more than capable of turning her over *his* knee.

She stepped closer to him and spoke for his ears alone. "If you desire to see what I wear beneath this dress—if anything at all—there *are* more pleasurable ways." She stepped back, smiling circumspectly as if they were discussing nothing more interesting than the canapés being passed by the waiters.

But Greg ruined that when he grabbed her elbow and nearly goose-stepped her right past Tanya's table, out the pool entrance and through the hidden doorway across the hall that led to the training room. Once there, he pressed her shoulders back against the door. "What game is this now, Kimi?"

She stomped down on the foolish excitement stampeding through her. "Do you see me laughing?"

He muttered an oath and pressed his mouth against hers.

She dropped the flute and fisted her fingers in his hair, kissing him back. Just as deeply. Just as frantically. Colors were swimming in her head when he finally dragged his lips to her cheek and she hauled in needful air.

"Tell me you've got something on under there." His mouth reached her neck. His fingers slid beneath one of the insubstantial straps. Drew it down her shoulder. The fabric dipped dangerously low over her breast. His other hand slid along the hem of the skirt, inching it higher along her bare thigh.

"Something," she admitted breathlessly.

He jerked back suddenly as if stung. Swearing ripely, he yanked his cell phone out of his pocket and she realized it was vibrating. He flipped the phone open. "Yeah. What?" His gaze sharpened on Kimi's face, and he slid her strap back where it belonged even as he snapped the phone closed and pocketed it once more. "Security," he muttered, rubbing his hand down his face.

"Is there a problem?"

He grimaced. "Nothing, other than that it took my director of security to remind me that we're not in the business of filming the staff's intimate escapades." He gestured at the discreet camera positioned well above their heads and focused on the doorway and corridor. Where they most clearly were standing.

She felt the blood drain out of her face. "How could I have forgotten the cameras?"

"How could *I?*" He pushed her back through the hidden doorway.

"All they w-would have seen was a, um, a kiss." His broad back would have blocked the way he had nearly drawn down her bodice. Drawn up the brief hem even higher over her thighs.

"A kiss is more than enough." He slapped the elevator call button and it immediately sighed open. He nudged her inside. "Go back to your room."

"What are you going to do?"

"Damage control," he muttered, and the doors shut, separating them.

Kimi stared at her mottled reflection in the elevator walls. She had wanted to get a reaction out of Greg—something to prove that she was not alone in her emotional upheaval. She had not intended for their—what could she even call their thwarted non-relationship?—to be broadcast via the hotel's closed-circuit system.

She ignored the elevator doors when they opened one floor down, and instead pushed the button for Jenny and

Richard's floor. She had not been on the twenty-first floor since she had left behind the Mahogany Suite nearly three weeks earlier.

Off the elevator, she turned the opposite direction from the Mahogany Suite and found her way to their suite. Mere seconds after her knock, Jenny pulled the door open. She eyed Kimi's appearance for a silent moment. "If Mori saw you in that dress he'd either send you to a nunnery or have a heart attack."

"Let us hope that he does not see it, then." She followed Jenny into the spacious suite. It was smaller than the Mahogany, but no less luxurious.

"I suppose that dress is one of Lana's creations." By Jenny's tone, she was clearly not a big fan.

"Yes. How is my nephew?"

Jenny's brow crinkled, but she took the change of subject. "Sleeping, thankfully. Richard took the train to Tokyo. He'll be back tomorrow." She waited a beat. "So what's wrong?"

Kimi shook her head and crossed to the windows. "Nothing." In the distance, she could see the lights of Kyoto Station. She dashed her fingers over her cheeks. "How are Dana and Harold?" To the outside world, some might think it unusual that the family had forged a relationship with Jenny's adoptive parents, but to Kimi it was simply normal.

"They're fine. What's wrong?"

"I told you. Nothing! Helen and Papa are arriving tomorrow, but when is the rest of the family coming in?"

"Pretty much everyone except Nina and David and their brood will be here for Christmas Day. Nina wanted to have Christmas morning for the kids in their own home, plus finish the last couple of nights of Chanukah. They'll be here for the New Year's gala, though. She says it'll be her last real trip before her pregnancy keeps her from traveling. Is something going on between you and Greg Sherman?"

Kimi whirled. "What?"

Jenny was lounging on the camel-colored sofa, her long copper-colored hair swept over her shoulder. "Is there?"

"Who said anything about Greg?"

"Nobody had to. A person only needs to be within ten feet of the two of you to feel the tension between you."

She hoped that it was only Jenny that seemed aware of that, and not everyone in the hotel. "He is not happy that I am working here," she admitted.

"Sweetheart, the tension I'm talking about doesn't have a thing to do with work."

Kimi felt her face flush at Jenny's dry tone. "He is not happy about that, either."

"Hmm."

She stepped out of her heels and folded her legs beneath her on the couch. "I have made such a mess of things, Jenny." She made a face and swiped at another tear. "I mean a *real* mess, this time. I thought I knew what I wanted; what was important. But now, now I don't know what I want. I don't know much of anything."

Jenny's gaze was steady on Kimi's face. "Are you sure about that?"

Kimi bit the inside of her lip. "I want what my father has with your mother," she admitted. "I want what you and Richard have." She wanted, some day, to be able to mark thirty years of love the way the Petersons were doing.

"And you've decided this in the few weeks since you've met Greg."

"How long after you met Richard did *you* know?"

Jenny's cheeks pinkened. "Point taken."

Kimi stared down at her hands. "How do you know if it is really love, though? What if it is just…just—"

"Sex?" Jenny provided gently.

"Yes."

"Are you afraid that it is?"

Kimi swallowed. "I fear that it is not."

Her sister leaned over and folded her in a hug. "Listen to your heart, Kimiko. That's the only advice I can give." A sudden wail from the other room had her straightening, though. "That would be my page."

Kimi unfolded her legs and stuffed her feet back into her killer heels. "Is it worth it, Jenny?"

Her sister rose, also. "Every second of every day," she assured softly.

Kimi sighed. "Go see to Jason. I will let myself out."

"You're going to be okay?"

Kimi nodded, though she was not sure of anything.

She took the guest elevator down to the fourth floor and tried not to feel as if the handful of people she passed was privy to her and Greg's lapse outside the training room. She did not know why it was so difficult now; she had been little more than a child when she had first become accustomed to people gossiping about her.

The door to Greg's room was closed when she passed it and she let herself into her own, only to stop short at the sight of him leaning against the side of her desk.

"I used a passkey," he said.

She slowly closed the door behind her. "I thought that was against your code of ethics."

"My ethics have taken a beating since you've come around."

She winced. "That was never my intention."

He sighed. "I know."

"You, um, you own jeans." It seemed a foolish observation once she voiced it. What did it matter that the very sexy *GQ* look he had sported at the party had been replaced by even more appealing worn blue jeans and a thick gray sweater?

"And I put them on one leg at a time," he drawled, though his face did not look particularly amused.

She did not need to have images of him dressing...or un-dressing...running through her imagination.

"Where have you been?"

She brushed her hands down the sides of the dress that she wished now she had left safely buried in her crowded closet. "I went up to see my stepsister. Did you, um, deal with the—"

"Sex tape?"

She flushed painfully. "Do not call it that! We were not—"

"Making out in the corridor of the hotel I run for your family?" His voice was tight. "That is exactly what we were doing, Kimi, and you'd damn well better believe that word about it is likely to spread."

"Can you not erase the tape or something?"

He flipped a small square device onto the desk. "It's a digital drive. And the only record that I know of."

"Why would there be one that you do not know of?"

"There shouldn't be. We were only lucky that Shin happened to be in the monitoring room to call and remind me that I'd lost all sense. And he can warn the other two guards who were there to keep their mouths shut, but that's a crapshoot at best."

"I am sorry I wore the dress."

He exhaled noisily. "It's not the damn dress, Kimi. It's *you*."

"Would you like me to apologize for being me?"

"That'd be like asking the earth to stop spinning. If word about this gets back to your parents, I'm done here."

"I wish I could convince you that you are wrong. If I called them right now and admitted the truth, you would see!"

"What truth? Not only am I your boss, I'm too damn old for you! You should be messing around with well-heeled college boys who are still wet behind the ears. Ones with pedigrees as long as my arm."

"I am not interested in college boys. Pedigreed or not. I am interested in you."

"Why?"

"I do not know!" Her voice rose with frustration. "You are uncompromising and annoying and—" her eyes were suddenly burning again "—and fair and honorable. And I—I am in love with you." There. She had said it. Voiced the words that had been hovering inside her for weeks now.

"Don't say that."

"*That* is the response every girl wants to hear," she observed, but inside her heart felt like it was cracking into pieces.

"What should I say?" he demanded roughly. "Should I go down on my knee and beg you to marry me?"

She could barely breathe. "Would that be s-so terrible?"

"Yes, because you'll come to your senses soon enough." His voice was flat. Uncompromising. "Particularly when it sinks in just how far apart our lives are. Then you'll realize that what you think might be—" his jaw tightened visibly "—*love* was anything but."

"The only thing that feels too far apart is you from me." She closed the space between them and slid her hands up his arms.

"Kimi, if we start this, I'm not going to be able to stop. Not again."

"When did I ever ask you to? You are the one who pulls away, Greg."

"Would you prefer I'd have taken you right there in the corridor for the camera to see?"

"You would not have done that."

He looked even more grim. "I'm glad you sound so certain, because I sure as hell am not." He caught her hands and squeezed them tightly for a moment, then set her from him.

His face could have been carved from stone, and wariness slid through her uneasily.

"I have to at least see the Taka through the gala."

The wariness shifted into full-blown alarm. "What do you mean?"

"I mean that after that, I'll be submitting my resignation to Helen and Mori."

"Do you not think that is a little extreme?" She tried for

lightness and fell miles short. The set look in those stained-glass eyes of his told her everything. "Greg." She lifted her hands, feeling utterly helpless. "You cannot resign. Not…not because of me. *I* will go."

"Your leaving wouldn't change what happened, Kimi."

"So you will give up what you have strived for all of your life just because we made love?" She stared into his face. "Or is that simply a convenient excuse for you to prove that you really do *not* belong in this world?"

The edge of his teeth bared. "I never said otherwise. I learned that a long time ago."

"From whom? That other *rich girl* you talked about?"

"Sydney was only a little taste," he said, his voice flat. "I've made a career in an industry where, in order to make it to the top, the only thing that matters is your pedigree. A pedigree I don't have and never will. The only thing I have is the stamp I've made on the houses I've run, and maybe, *maybe* some day that would stand well enough to open my own. If I'm lucky. If I had the financing. If I had a spotless reputation that could make up even partially for having the gall to even try. Believe me, Kimi. Working in this world is not the same as belonging to it."

"And because I do belong to it, you and I—" she waved her hand dismissively "—can never have anything other than an, an *interlude*."

"An interlude I should have never allowed."

"Why not? At least you can use it as an excuse to flog yourself even more!"

"You don't know what the hell you're talking about."

Anger, like none she had ever known, slammed into her. "Really? How about the fact that I know exactly how to find any and every excuse to avoid finishing something important. I know about setting my own bombs to go off before I can even cross the bridge of something that matters, because it is so much easier to stay in place than to start across and chance failure at the other side!" She lifted her chin, though she was trembling from head to foot, and pointed her finger in his face. "You want to open your own hotels, Greg? Maybe you should start learning your lessons from Helen. She doesn't have your almighty important pedigree, and look where she is. She takes her chances because something matters to her. If you want to blow off the trust my parents have put in you to helm this hotel, that is your business, Greg. But do not *dare* to use me as an excuse. All of us deserve better. Including you."

The muscle in his jaw worked but she did not back down. Did not back away.

After a long, tense silence, he walked through the connecting doorway and quietly closed the door behind him.

It felt as if a door had closed inside her heart, as well.

Chapter Eleven

"Merry Christmas, Greg." Helen Taka-Hanson personally answered his knock on the Presidential Suite's door. "I'm so pleased you're able to join us for dinner tonight. I love a big Christmas get-together. Kimi warned me that you might be too busy with your duties. I'm glad that wasn't the case." She swung the door wide. "Aren't those lovely?"

Greg handed her the arrangement of fresh flowers. "They pale next to you, I'm afraid."

She smiled widely. "Such a smooth tongue. Come in, come in." He felt like hell and wanted to be there the way he wanted a throbbing hole in his head. No matter how closely Kimi's words had struck him, he felt completely out of place. Whether Helen recognized the resistance inside him at joining the Takas for this private dinner or not, she tucked her arm through his and drew him across the threshold.

The Presidential Suite—all 3,200 square feet of it—was

decked to the nines with holiday cheer and tall, slender Helen Taka-Hanson, dressed in muted gold from head to toe, looked like she should be the angel atop the decorated nine-foot Christmas tree that took center stage.

"As you can see, we've made ourselves quite at home since we arrived yesterday." Her grin was slightly impish and somewhat at odds with her overwhelmingly classic beauty.

"I see that." He eyed the enormous tree. It had not been present when he'd personally shown Helen and Mori to their suite the previous day. It was then that Helen had issued her insistent invitation for Christmas dinner.

He tried not to eye Kimi, who was kneeling next to the tree.

Not that she was looking at him. She hadn't said two words to him since he'd walked out of her room the other night. Like the coward he was, he'd done his share of avoiding her, too. But her heartfelt words haunted him constantly.

I am in love with you.

"It's quite a display," he managed to tell Helen over the memory of Kimi's voice. "It puts the decorations we have in the lobby to shame."

"The decorations around the hotel are most becoming," Helen assured. She let go of Greg's arm and crossed the room. "Would you like a cocktail?" She rummaged behind the granite-topped bar and came up with a Waterford pitcher that she turned into an impromptu vase for the flowers.

"Whatever you're having would be fine." Greg's gaze crept over to Kimi again. She wore a deep blue off-the-shoulder dress that clung from just below the curve of her shoulders to her knees. Cashmere, most likely.

Soft. But not as soft as he knew her skin was.

"It is my wife's one requirement of Christmas," Mori Taka said, delivering the wine glass to Greg.

Greg dragged his focus from Kimi to her father. He wasn't quite as tall as Greg, but he was just as broad. Not a guy to cross either in the boardroom or on the streets.

"Whenever we travel over the holidays, Helen insists on putting up a tree and decorating it with the ornaments she has collected over the years," Mori continued, amused. His English was more accented than Kimi's, but only barely.

"Collected or made." Helen went to the tree and touched a glittering, elongated star. "Kimi made this when she was sixteen."

"Her artist phase," Mori added, casting an indulgent look toward his daughter.

Greg could remember making ornaments in school and taking them to whatever dump they were currently calling home. But only once or twice could he recall there being a tree to hang them on. He knew that Mona had never bothered trying to save any of his efforts.

"My family could bore you with recounting all of my *phases*," Kimi said, not looking at him. She adjusted the position of yet another package.

A chime sounded. "Excuse me a moment." Helen headed back to the foyer.

"Kimi-chan, do you plan to shake and rattle every package beneath the tree? Mr. Sherman will think you have no patience at all."

Greg could feel the reluctance rolling off her in waves, but she rose smoothly to her feet and smiled at her father. "I shake only those that have my name on the tag, Papa." She turned toward Greg, though her gaze rose no higher than his chin. "And Mr. Sherman is already aware of my impatient nature, are you not, Mr. Sherman?"

"Zest for life, Ms. Taka."

At that, Kimi flashed him a skeptical glance.

I am in love with you. Maybe her zest had gotten out of hand. He'd warned her she hadn't meant it. Maybe she hadn't.

"Good heavens, all this mister and miss business sounds entirely too formal for a Christmas get-together," Helen observed, returning with her daughter and son-in-law in tow.

Jenny's coloring was different than Helen's—she was a redhead, for one thing—but seeing the two women standing alongside one another, their resemblance was even more striking.

"Mr. Sherman's professionalism has made an indelible habit," Kimi said. She crossed to her sister. "May I take him?"

Jenny passed over the baby, murmuring something he couldn't hear before Kimi wandered away from the crowd, cooing to the small bundle.

Greg finally looked away from her, only to find Mori watching him. His fingers tightened around the stem of the wine glass. "I'm sorry I was unable to give you a tour of the Taka yesterday afternoon, myself."

"Perfectly understandable. You have responsibilities," Mori dismissed smoothly. "Carter Janes was more than informative."

The back of Greg's neck itched. Just how informative would his assistant manager have been? Shin had already alerted Greg to the few rumblings he'd heard where Greg and Kimi were concerned. Rumblings that he'd reportedly squelched.

For all the good that was likely to do.

"You're doing an excellent job, Greg," Helen said. "Mori and I couldn't be more pleased, isn't that right, darling?"

"As usual, my wife has found the right notes for success."

That music would come to a screeching halt once they knew about Greg and Kimi. "I look forward to going over the final details for the gala on New Year's Eve." Final details that would be including his resignation, if Greg made it even that long, considering the unreadable look on Mori's face.

"All right. That is enough business for tonight," Helen ordered lightly. "We'll have plenty of time after today to discuss it all." The door chime rang again. "Kimi, darling, would you mind?"

Looking altogether too natural for comfort with the baby in her arms, Kimi went to answer the door, and soon the living area was crowded with even more family members as the influx didn't seem to stop through one glass of wine or the next.

"The boys," as Helen called them, were her fully adult stepsons from her first marriage to millionaire George Hanson. Some of them Greg had met before. Some not. Jack was the eldest. Another legal eagle like Richard Warren. Then came Evan and Andrew with their wives and their assortment of young offspring.

Before long, the place was a hive of activity. They could have been any rambunctious, somewhat disorderly family from anywhere—squabbling over everything from football to politics to favorite shoe designers. It probably should have seemed odd that they were there in the Presidential Suite.

But, Greg realized, it wasn't odd at all.

It was...enviable.

And he didn't belong there at all, no matter how graciously Helen had insisted he join them for their dinner.

He finished the wine that Mori had refilled more than once, escaping a heated debate between Evan and Andrew over what teams were shoo-ins for the Super Bowl, and took the glass over to the bar.

"Running away already?" Kimi's voice was low, barely audible over the voices and laughter and Christmas carols playing from the state-of-the-art sound system.

"Don't you think it's wise?"

She pressed the baby's small hand to her lips. He'd noticed that she hadn't let go of the infant once since she'd taken him from his mother. "You already know exactly what I think."

"This is a family affair. I'm not family."

"You could be."

He very nearly snapped the wineglass stem in two. "Kimi—"

"*Sumimasen.* Please. Forget I said that." Her cheeks were red. "Blame it on the wine."

"I have yet to see you carrying a wineglass since I arrived. Your hands have mostly been full of your nephew."

"Then blame it on whatever you like. Maybe I just have weddings on the brain since the Nguyens' fete."

Business. Talk about business. "I heard you handled everything brilliantly. I would have told you earlier if I'd had a chance." If he hadn't been avoiding her.

She lifted a shoulder. "We all have our jobs to do. I am surprised to see you here this evening, though. Unless you are planning to confess all to them over the Christmas pudding."

His jaw tightened. "No."

"Then why come?"

"It's hard to refuse an invitation from the owners."

She looked up at him through her lashes. "Is that the only reason?"

"Remember, now, no business talk over there." Helen's voice carried over the others.

"Then what else would we talk about?" Kimi smiled lightly, raising her voice enough to be heard. "Mr. Sherman was enquiring about a large wedding we held here the evening before last."

"Did you jump out of the cake?" Andrew asked, amused. "Hold on. That would have been the bachelor party."

Kimi made a face at him. "Very funny. I was in charge of the event."

Andrew visibly shuddered, earning himself an elbow poke from his petite wife. *"What?"*

"Be nice," Delia chided.

"Oh, hell. Kimi knows I'm just kidding, don't you, squirt?"

Kimi just kissed the baby's tiny knuckles again, looking amused and immune to the teasing.

Greg saw it for the act that it was, though. "The wedding had a guest list of four hundred," he told them. "And Kimi was the only person in the house able to satisfy the exacting demands of the wedding coordinator. She did an excellent job. The event was flawless, according to the Nguyens. It's a guarantee that we'll have more business out of it. The bride's father is a well-known Japanese artist. I met with him this afternoon to discuss some photography he'd like to do of the hotel."

"This afternoon?" Delia looked surprised. "But it's Christmas Day."

"Yet still a workday for most in Japan," Kimi reminded. Her gaze wouldn't meet his. "And did I tell you that I want a raise?"

Everyone laughed.

Everyone but Greg and Kimi.

And Kimi's father, Greg realized, seeing the tall man from the corner of his eyes.

Fortunately, Helen announced that dinner was served, and in the mass exodus to the formal dining room, the awkwardness passed. Also what passed was Greg's opportunity to make an easy escape, and he found himself seated between Jack and his gregarious wife, Samantha.

Kimi was across the table, several chairs down.

That ought to have made enjoying the meal personally prepared by Chef Lorenzo an easy task.

Instead, the food tasted like straw, and he kept watching Kimi, waiting and sweating like some besotted idiot for her to look his way. But she didn't. Instead, she stayed busy holding her own among the general teasing she continued to get, particularly from her stepbrothers who treated her as if she were still an incorrigible schoolgirl instead of the grown woman she'd become.

The meal seemed like it would never end, but of course it did, and when everyone meandered back into the living room, taking up one spot or another around the enormous tree, he thought his escape was at last in sight. It was apparent that this family Christmas celebration was complete all the way down to gift exchanges.

He quickly started making the appropriate thanks to his host and hostess for their hospitality, but Helen squashed his notion of working his way to the door. "Kimi, scoot over so Greg can sit on the couch, too."

"Really, Helen, I should be getting back—"

"—to where?" In complete disregard for her couture, she sat

down on the floor right next to the Christmas tree. "We've seen for ourselves just how capable your assistant manager is, now be a good boy and sit."

Greg heard the muffled sound Kimi made. She scooted, though, and he reluctantly took the spot she cleared.

Andrew, on the other side of her, leaned over, grinning. "Look out, Greg. You've earned your way into being one of Helen's *boys*. It's a phrase that tends to stick no matter how old we get."

"Of course *we* keep getting older," Evan added from his perch on the arm of the chair where his wife, Meredith, sat. "But the women in this family just all stay the same."

"And what is wrong with that?" Helen grinned. She began checking gift tags on the wrapped packages beneath the tree and doled them out with the panache of a Las Vegas dealer.

When Greg ended up with an oversized box on his lap, he immediately started to pass it on.

"No, no, Greg." Helen barely hesitated in her activity. "That one's yours."

Kimi, miraculously having managed to keep several inches of space between them on the silk-covered couch, ruined the effort by leaning her shoulder against his side to look for herself at the small tag nearly obscured by an enormous gold bow. "'To Greg. Best regards from Helen and Mori'. I guess that says it all." She retreated to her space.

It annoyed the hell out of him that he wanted to scoop her back against his side once again.

"You really shouldn't have," he told Kimi's parents.

Helen just smiled and waved off the sentiment. "If someone doesn't begin opening gifts, we're *never* going to get to bed tonight."

"Forget that," Andrew drawled, giving his wife a meaningful look. He tore into one of his packages.

"Open it."

Greg eyed Kimi. "Do you know what it is?"

She shook her head. "That is the point of opening a present, Greg," she offered mildly. "To see what is inside."

"I don't have anything for them in return."

"Another point about gifts. They are freely given with no expectation in return." Her mild facade broke momentarily, and she looked away, busying herself with rearranging the assortment of boxes and festive bags around her feet. When she straightened, she held a narrow wrapped item. "Here is another." She thrust it toward him. "Merry Christmas."

He could tell by the shape that it was a CD. "What is it?"

She sighed a little and wiggled the disc. The shiny white curls of ribbon on top of it bounced. "What did I just say about opening gifts? Do not worry. I just thought it would be something you might enjoy."

He took it from her. "I don't have anything for you, either." He should have been more prepared.

It *was* Christmas.

He'd just never really celebrated the holiday in the normal way before. Ordinarily, he was the one on the job, leaving all the festivities to those who had people in their lives that mattered.

"I did not expect anything from you." She frowned. "That did not sound right."

Considering the situation between them—the situation that he should have known enough to avoid in the first place—he figured it sounded pretty much "right."

But sitting there in the middle of her family was not exactly the place where he wanted to get into that debate. Particularly when she'd already blasted him with her own particular take on it.

I am in love with you.

The words circled inside his head again with all the delicacy of a jackhammer.

He cleared his dry throat and slid the crisscrossed mass

of ribbons off Kimi's gift and turned it over, finding the taped edge.

She made a muffled sound. "I should have known you were one of *those*."

"Those?"

"The type who unfastens every fold, who never shreds the paper, never rips a ribbon."

"While you're the type to impetuously tear it all apart to get at what is inside."

Barely an inch of bare shoulder showed above the clinging dress, but it was an inch that still managed to torment him as she shrugged slightly. "Look around you," she suggested. "It is part of the fun."

Certainly, most of her family was tearing into their gifts with what looked like sheer abandon. Strips of wrapping paper in every color and pattern were strewn about, shining ribbons and bows were being batted around like tennis balls.

"Some of us prefer to savor the anticipation." He slid his finger beneath the paper, coaxing the adhesive free.

Her lovely throat worked in a swallow, and her eyes seemed to darken even more. "I like anticipation, too," she murmured huskily. "As well as the…culmination."

The paper suddenly ripped beneath his finger.

Kimi smiled faintly, looking as satisfied as a sleek cat. "It is nice to see that you are not always in control."

It was a good thing that she didn't know just how uncontrolled he did feel where she was concerned. But tearing the paper accomplished one thing. He could clearly see that the item was indeed a CD. "Who is it?"

"Just a CD I managed to find for you."

He peeled away the rest of the wrapping paper, looking at the label with no small amount of surprise. "The children's orchestra?" He eyed her. "I didn't realize they'd had anything recorded. That's what they were doing all the concerts for; to raise money so that they could get out a recording."

"It was very recent." She busied herself with selecting a package to pull onto her lap.

His suspicion was swift. "Kimi. What did you do?"

She gave him an innocent look that wouldn't have bought a cup of coffee. "I don't know what you mean." She tore open the package on her lap and tossed the paper onto the growing collection of it in the center of the floor. The box quickly followed, while she held up the pink blouse she'd extracted to her shoulders. "It is lovely, Meredith. Thank you."

Across the room, Meredith grinned. "I overruled Evan's choice of a stuffed koala bear."

"I appreciate that."

"I thought you liked stuffed animals," Evan complained. "God knows you always had enough of 'em in your bedroom. And it *was* from Australia when Meredith and I were there."

Kimi rolled her eyes and picked up her next gift. Greg, however, couldn't get past the CD. Beneath the cover of wrapping paper and packages, he closed his hand over hers. "Did you arrange the recording?"

She looked startled, then slid her hand free. "I made a phone call," she allowed.

"To whom?"

"Kobayashi Media saw the value in making a gift to the orchestra's fund." She toyed with the velvety red bow atop her package. "And, um, my grandfather saw fit to match it."

"When?"

"The recording was made last week at Kyoto University."

"I meant when did you do this? Why didn't you tell me?"

"After we heard their concert. I…I did not want you to think I did it merely to gain your approval. The children's orchestra was just something that seemed to matter to you." She cast a quick glance at his face. "You should open your other gift," she prompted. "Everyone is nearly through."

Everyone but her. Despite her contention that she was the rip-and-tear type.

He was a lot more interested in her than the gift from Helen and Mori, but he quickly unfolded the gold wrapping paper to reveal an extremely fine, leather attaché. His initials, along with the Taka insignia were engraved on the locking clasps.

It was a well-chosen executive type of gift. One that made him feel like a fraud. "Looks like I should be able to retire my old briefcase," he told Helen. "Thank you both."

Helen looked thoroughly pleased and satisfied sitting there in the midst of her family. Mori, sitting in the chair behind her, had his hand on her shoulder. His expression was much more difficult to read, but he, too, looked content.

Beside him, Kimi had pushed aside all of her packages but one. Looking suddenly nervous, she rose and stepped through the debris. "I have one more gift for you and Helen, Papa." She handed the velvet bow-topped parcel to him.

"What is it?" Mori asked.

Kimi let out a soft exclamation, glancing back at Greg. What was it about the men in her life? "Between the two of you—" she broke off, shaking her head. Greg had made it plain that he did not want to be in her life. "Open and see."

Her father's gaze narrowed on her face. He began to slowly pick open the paper but Helen tsked and reached up to rip it away, leaving Mori to lift off the top of the box.

Then he went still, looking at the contents. Helen went up on her knees to look, as well. "Oh, my—" She suddenly jumped to her feet, closing her arms around Kimi in a swift hug. "It's your college diploma!"

Her father rose more slowly. He set aside the box, only to have it snatched up by Jack, who pulled out the diploma Tanya had helped her get matted and framed. "I thought you quit." He handed off the frame to his wife who handed it off to Meredith.

"I went back." Kimi stated the obvious.

"You should have told us." Her father looked down at her, clearly suspicious.

"If I had told you, I would not have been able to surprise you."

"Hai. After everything it most assuredly would have been a surprise."

"Oh, Mori." Helen clasped Kimi's face in her hands. "Is that the only reason you finished? As a surprise to please us?"

"At first." Of all the eyes in the room, Kimi felt Greg's most keenly. This is what she got for making such a public announcement. "But somewhere along the way, I realized I *wanted* to finish. For me."

Helen smiled. Her green eyes were soft. "And that, my darling, is the very best reason."

"Were you working here at all, then?" Mori asked.

She tried to squelch her surge of defensiveness. "Of course I was."

"Then how did you have time to make up your classes?"

So much for squelching. "What do you think I did, Papa? Forge my own diploma? This is not junior high school. I have not changed a D to a B to avoid your wrath."

"She did her class work when she was off duty," Greg answered, before she could lose her composure altogether. "Which wasn't all that often considering all the times she's pitched in wherever we needed someone."

She turned around to face him. "I do not need you to fight my battles, Greg."

He rose from the couch, still holding the CD. "Good, because I don't intend to." He eyed Mori. "Your daughter has become a valued member of my staff. She's everything you should wish for in a representative of the Taka hotels. And while I have no right to be, I'm still proud of the work she's done here."

"I am pleased to hear your opinion," Mori told Greg evenly. "But I think this is a family matter, now."

"Papa!"

But it was too late.

"Of course." Greg tilted his head slightly. "Thank you, again, Helen, for your hospitality this evening. I wish you all a merry holiday. Everyone here at the hotel is, of course, at your disposal." With that utterly practiced, smooth smile that he had, he walked out of the suite.

Silence reigned, broken only by Helen. "Well. I cannot imagine what he thinks about us now."

Kimi could imagine. "He thinks he is not good enough for us," she said huskily. "And you—" she turned on her father "—have given him proof of it."

Her father's eyebrows drew together. "*What* are you talking about?"

"Maybe we all should give Kimi some privacy with Helen and Mori," Jenny announced hurriedly. "It's long past time that Richard and I got Jason into his crib for the night."

"Do not run away on my account," Kimi said. "I'm leaving, anyway."

"Oh, Kimi." Helen's concern was plainly evident as she stood between Kimi and Mori. "Don't hurry off, too. This is such a thing to celebrate. You've finished college!"

"And I thought that if I did, you would allow me to come back to Chicago and work there."

Her father's lips thinned. "Returning to Chicago was always your choice, Kimiko."

Her lips parted, disbelieving. "Right. With my tail tucked because I managed to fail you, yet again. That is what you expected. I thought if I could find my place within the family business, the way the boys have, that it would no longer matter to you that I was not the very proper *Japanese* daughter you always wanted. But you know what, Papa? I no longer worry about failing you. Or failing myself because someone might see beyond the almighty Taka-glitter to the very ordinary person that I am inside. What matters is doing your best. Trying. And I learned *that* working for the man who just walked out of here!"

"He is an excellent manager," Mori said stiffly.

"Yes, he is," Kimi said swiftly. "And he is also the man I love."

Silence, broken only by Andrew's faint "Whoa," and Delia's quiet "shush," followed.

Kimi faced her parents, head-on. Mori, typically, looked fierce and disapproving. Helen, also typically, looked concerned. "Does Greg share your feelings," she finally asked.

"I don't know," Kimi admitted painfully.

Helen cast a quick look up at Mori. "But the two of you are...involved? Personally?"

"It is not a schoolgirl crush," Kimi assured quietly. More than that, she had no intention of saying. "I think I have had all the celebrating I can stand for one night." She glanced around, taking in the varying expressions of shock on her family's faces. "I'm sorry if I have ruined your Christmas celebration."

"Oh, Kimi," Helen murmured. "You've never ruined anything."

But Kimi was already walking out the door.

Chapter Twelve

In her room, Kimi pulled open her side of the connecting door and knocked softly. "Greg? Please open the door."

Silence.

She leaned her forehead against the smooth wood. "I am not going to give up."

More silence.

She could not even be certain that he was *in* his room.

She picked up the phone and rang his room. Through the door she could faintly hear it ringing on his side.

But no answer.

She tossed down the phone and went back to the door, knocking again. "If you ever want some peace, Greg, open the door."

It suddenly yanked open, and she nearly tumbled into his room. He caught her shoulders, keeping her from landing on him. "Peace? That's a good one. What do you want, Kimi?"

You. She managed to keep the thought to herself. "I wanted to see if you were all right."

His lips twisted, and he let go of her, turning away. "Touching. But I've been taking care of myself since long before you were bouncing on your daddy's knee."

She followed him into his room. Despite the similarities to her own, it was distinctively his space, and she could not help casting a painfully curious look around it. From what she could see, he displayed no personal effects at all. No photos. No mementos. Just a small stack of books on his nightstand and a pile of what looked like professional journals and newspapers scattered on his desk. "I am sorry for what my father said."

"Why?" He leaned back against the desk, crossing his arms and making the fine weave of his shirt strain at the shoulders. "I wouldn't want my family matters aired to all and sundry, either."

"You are hardly *all and sundry*. And if he had wanted a private conversation, he could have been more polite about it."

"Your father is Mori Taka. He doesn't have to worry about offending anyone with his bluntness."

"He did offend you, then."

He let out a sigh. "No. Kimi, I understand your father perfectly well. I understand his position, and God knows I understand mine."

"That is more than I can say, then." She pressed her hands together. "I...told them how I...how I feel about you."

His jaw tightened. He shoved his hand through his hair. "A great time for you to decide not to keep anything else secret from them. Your father probably has some Samurai sword he keeps under his bed for just these situations."

"You need not fear my father."

"Fearing and having a healthy respect for him ain't the same thing, honey."

No. She supposed that fear had not been the correct word. "Helen asked if you shared my feelings. I told her I did not know."

He watched her silently.

"It, um, it is okay if you do not," she added hurriedly. A blatant lie if ever there was one. "I would just r-rather know."

"I warned you that there would never be anything more." His voice was deep. Low.

"That is not what I asked, Greg."

"It's the only answer you're getting."

"I know you feel something for me." She stepped closer. "I can see it in your eyes when you look at me."

"Then what the hell are you asking me for?" Irritation drew his brows together. "It doesn't matter what I feel, Kimi."

"I think it is the only thing that matters."

"Spoken like the young woman that you are."

She laid her palm along his jaw. It was hot against her palm. "And you still have not answered me. I can only wonder why? If you felt nothing, you would simply say so."

He caught her fingers in his, squeezing them. "I want you in my bed," he said flatly.

She frowned, realizing that his hand was as hot as his jaw. She pressed her other hand to his face. "You are burning up."

"Did you hear what I said?"

"I heard." She moved her palm to his forehead. "You are ill. Why did you not say something?"

"I'm not ill," he groused.

She made a face. "Lie down. I will get a cold cloth for your forehead."

"Damn it, Kimi, I don't want your coddling."

"You do not want anything from me outside of the bed. I get it." She planted her hands on his iron midsection and shoved him toward the bed. Surprise was on her side, and he took an unsteady step back, only to find the bed behind his shins, and he went down like a ton of bricks. She pointed her finger at him. "Stay there."

He grimaced. "You're pretty full of orders all of a sudden."

"Fire me for insubordination." Her voice was flat. "It would solve all of our problems." She went into his bathroom. It was a mirror image of hers, right down to the artistically arranged display of bath linens on the stone shelf alongside the granite counter. Except for the shaving paraphernalia and the bottle of his aftershave, anyway.

She ignored the desire to open the aftershave to inhale his scent and snatched up a washcloth, ran it beneath the faucet and returned to his bedside.

Miraculously—or perhaps just in proof that he really did *not* feel well—he had stayed put.

"Here." She held out the dripping cloth.

He ignored it. "I don't need that. I told you. I'm fine."

"Of course you are. That is why you have an obvious fever." She hiked her knee on the mattress and leaned over him to dump the cloth over his forehead for herself. "Did you get one of your flu shots that you were nagging the rest of us to get?"

"Did *you* go up that day I had the clinic set up?"

"I was in Nesutotaka that day," she reminded. "Catering to my grandfather's whims so that *your* mayor's luncheon was better attended."

He lifted the cloth off his eyes, giving her a baleful look. "I didn't ask for that particular sacrifice," he pointed out. "And you're dripping water all over me."

"You are a big boy. Did you get the shot or not?" She snatched the cloth from his fingers and replaced it, holding it there with her hand lest he try to evade it again. "You need to cool off."

"Yes, I did, and there *is* no cooling off," he muttered. "The daily cold showers I've been reduced to these past few weeks have proven that."

She ignored the part inside her that clenched hard in response to that revelation. "We need a thermometer."

"No, we don't."

"I bet you were a trial to your mother when you were young and not feeling well."

"My mother was a trial to me." Without rising from the bed, he started to toe off his shoes.

She left the wet cloth in place and slid off the bed. "Let me help."

Greg lifted the edge of the cloth that was dripping water down his face and eyed her. She tucked his foot against her flat abdomen with no regard whatsoever for the fine cashmere of her dress, and with great seriousness attacked his shoelaces.

His head was pounding, his throat was raw and he was so abruptly turned on that it took every speck of self-control not to reach for her. Instead, he just lay there while she pulled off his shoes and tossed them aside. "I don't get sick," he said.

She made a mocking sound. "How manly of you." The bed barely moved from her slight body when she climbed back up beside him. Her fingers settled on his shirt and began working at the buttons.

"Whoa." He tossed aside the dripping cloth and sat up. "What are you doing?"

Her expression was uncommonly patient. "Is something wrong?"

"I can take off my own shirt."

She folded her hands in her lap. "All right."

"You don't have to sit here and watch me!"

"Such modesty. Does it make you nervous?" She gave an exasperated sigh and slid off the bed. "Fine. Where is your aspirin?"

"I don't have any."

She tsked. "Good thing that I do. But when I return, you had better be properly in bed."

"I'm quaking in my boots."

"You are not wearing any." She padded out of the room, and he wearily threw off the rest of his clothes and climbed into bed.

"Now I know you must be miserable," she said when she returned, bearing a glass of water. "You actually did what I said." She perched beside him and dropped a few white pills into his palm.

He tossed back the aspirin and leaned back against the cool pillow.

"How long have you been this way?" She found the washcloth again and folded it against his forehead.

"A couple of days. I thought I could shake it off. The fever's new." He sighed, pressing his hand over hers against the cloth, as much to feel her as to feel more of the coolness it offered.

"Not a very fun way to spend Christmas." Her soft voice seemed as soothing as her hand.

"I've had worse." He thought of Helen's display in the Presidential Suite versus the meager holidays of his childhood. "None of them were ever like yours, that's for sure."

"What were they like?" She managed to lay herself alongside him, and he didn't have the energy to protest.

At least that was the reason he gave himself. Which didn't excuse him folding his arm around her, or sinking his fingers into her cool, silky hair. He was *supposed* to be keeping his distance from her. "They were like most any other day. Mona looking for her next high. Me looking for our next meal."

"Oh, Greg."

"Don't get all sympathetic and gooey."

"I would not dare."

He lifted the edge of the washcloth. "You're humoring me."

"Perhaps a little." She pressed her lips to his cheek.

"I'm probably contagious. I'll be responsible for sending the plague through your entire family."

"And people accuse me of being melodramatic." She pressed the cloth back in place. "What is your mother like now? Aside from sending you…medicinal…herbs? By the way, I can attest to their effectiveness."

He exhaled. "Honey, that wasn't herbs. That was *you*." What *was* Mona like now? "She's been clean and sober five years now. I had to get her into rehab three different times to accomplish it."

"But she *did* accomplish it," Kimi pointed out.

Unlike her mother, who'd succumbed in the most final of ways. "She's clean, and maybe it'll stick, but she's got no idea how to handle her life. She's tootling around Europe right now with some guy she met in a parking lot."

"But is she happy?"

He grimaced. "How could she be?"

"Perhaps for her, finishing something is not the important part of life." Her voice was calm. "It is the journey, not the destination, and all that."

"Good thing," he muttered. "Only, her journeys are mostly abbreviated pit stops."

"Did you invite her to the grand opening gala?"

He grimaced. "Yes." He'd sent plane tickets, too. Which he knew wouldn't be used. "She won't come."

"You sound very certain."

"I know Mona." And he'd accepted that some things—some people—couldn't be changed.

"It is no wonder why you are Mr. Responsible. You have had to be."

"Don't go making more of it than it was, Kimi. I learned early on that I liked my creature comforts. So I found a way to get 'em."

"Mmm-hmm." Her fingers stroked over his neck. "And to take care of her, I'll bet. Go to sleep. You will feel better in the morning."

"You're beside me on my bed. You think I want to sleep?"

She started to move away. "Then I will go to my own room now."

"Don't." He tightened his grip, and she subsided once more against his side. His fingers slid through her hair, blindly stroking it down over her shoulder, meeting the edge of that soft, clinging dress. "I didn't tell you how pretty you look in blue."

"Maybe I should call the doctor. Your fever has you being entirely too sweet."

He started to snort, only to grimace at the rawness in his throat. "I know. I'm a bastard."

"No." Her fingertips strayed up, over his lips. "I am a smart aleck."

"That's true."

She lightly tapped his cheek. "Do you want me to lie beside you, or not?"

His fingers found their way beneath the cashmere. "You always look good. Even in that ridiculous excuse of a skirt that first day."

"I will convey your exuberant praise to my friend Lana."

"Were you really wearing anything at all under that dress?" He didn't have to elaborate more than that; she knew good and well what dress he meant.

"Greg." She shifted against him. "I don't think now is the time to—"

"I'm a dying man here, Kimi."

She pressed her head against his jaw. "You are more like an incorrigible boy at the moment, and sadly, I find it amazingly irresistible."

"Were you?"

She lifted her head. Moistened her lips. "A…a new belly ring. It has a, um, a small monogrammed charm on it."

"Your father should shoot me," he muttered. "It'd put us both out of our misery." He shouldn't have asked. "Is *that* all?" He definitely shouldn't ask that. He was already too damned hot.

"Use your imagination."

He dragged the washcloth off his face and pitched it off the side of the bed. It felt nearly as hot as he did. It would take a snow bank to cool him off. "I'm sorry I asked."

"As well you should be." The bed barely moved when she left it. Moments later, she returned, with the washcloth wet and cool again. Standing beside the bed, she handed it to him. "Here."

"You're not going to mop my brow?"

Her hair tumbled in tangled strands around her shoulders. Tangles that his fingers had caused. "For a sick man you are managing to summon a lot of attitude."

"Are you wearing that new monogrammed charm thing right now?"

Her long, lovely throat worked. "I should go into my own room so that you will stop this jabbering and go to sleep."

"I'd rather you stay." And not just to show him the new jewel glinting against her navel.

Her lashes swept down, hiding those dark eyes that drowned him in his dreams. "Which you would never admit if you were not feverish. It is nearly midnight, Greg. Get some rest."

He grimaced. "Merry Christmas to you, too."

"Do not grouse." She leaned over and pressed her lips to his forehead. Over his eyes. Barely grazed against his mouth. "Merry Christmas, Greg."

He caught her shoulders before she could straighten. "Why can't I get you out of my head, Kimiko Taka?"

Her eyes were wide. "Don't worry, Greg. I will leave here as soon as a replacement can be found."

"There *is* no replacement." He grimaced. "Damn it." Because he was weak, he pulled her down onto the bed beside him again. "Humor me."

"I thought you did not want that."

"I want *you*."

"Don't sound so delighted about it," she murmured, but she'd stopped straining against him and turned on her side, tucking herself against him as if they'd been sleeping that way for eons.

He worked the comforter out from between them, leaving only the sheet, and scooped her closer. The soft nape of her neck was more of a balm to his feverish skin than any wet washcloth could ever be. "Is it a *K* or a *T*?"

"What?"

He splayed his hand across her flat abdomen. "The monogram."

She was silent for so long he thought she wouldn't answer. "It is a *G*. Carved in a tiny piece of jade."

He weathered the blast of that. But it wasn't easy. "How old were you when you pierced your belly button?"

He felt her deep sigh. "Sixteen. When my father found out he was livid. Helen convinced him it was better than a tattoo, since a ring can always be removed."

"I'd be livid if my daughter pierced her navel, too." But there was definitely something about hers that got under his skin.

"You said you were too ancient to consider daughters or sons."

He dragged his fingers along her flat belly until he felt the faint indent of her navel. "You're wearing it now, aren't you?" His voice was low.

She exhaled. Finally whispered a soft "yes."

He felt parched in a way that had nothing to do with an elevated temperature.

She lifted her head suddenly, looking over her shoulder at him. "I thought you were feeling ill. You are—" She blushed. This woman who could walk into a room of three hundred people wearing that naked dress.

"Hard." His lips twisted. "Believe me. I know." He didn't bother pulling back from the sweet curve of her rear. The sheet and her cashmere dress was not much of a barrier, but it was enough. "It'll go away." In a couple of decades. "Thank for the CD."

She lowered her head again. Her fingers slid through his and she brushed her lips against the inside of his wrist. "You are welcome. Go to sleep."

He reached back and hit the light switch next to the bed, dousing the room into darkness but for the faint glow coming from Kimi's room.

His hands slid along her hip. Slowly inched along the cashmere. Felt the gentle rise of her hip. The taut slope of her thigh.

She caught his wandering hand in hers. "Stop that."

"Do you want kids, Kimi?"

"Why? If I say that I do, you will either tell me I am too young to know my own mind, or warn me not to include the idea of you and children in the same thought."

He couldn't deny it. "I'm too old to start a family."

"Yes." She drew out the word and managed to wriggle even closer to him. "Thirty-two *is* decrepit."

"I was right when I said Mori never spanked you, wasn't I?"

"He did not need to. All he needed to do was give me that very stern look of his, and I knew I was done for."

"He probably gave you one hellacious look after I left tonight."

"He did. For once it did not have the usual effect. Maybe that means I have grown up at last."

While he felt like a green youth in the god-awful throes of first love. He blamed the escape of that particular notion on the deep ache inside his head.

It couldn't be the ache inside his chest.

"Don't let anyone kid you, Kimiko. Age is not necessarily an indicator of maturity."

"If you are not going to go to sleep, then I am going to my own room." But she made no move to go.

He was glad. "I don't want you quitting your job because of me."

"I do not want you to quit your job for any reason, most especially me." She drew his hand up to her heart. "If things were different—"

"They aren't." This time he was the one to say the words. "Go to sleep, Kimi."

She exhaled. Her slender form was warm and soft against him. He knew she was just as wide awake as he was, but she said no more.

And finally, wrapped together, they both slept.

* * *

"Mori. It is just a picture. It means nothing." Helen eyed her husband over their intimate breakfast table.

He slapped the newspaper down on the table between them. A grainy photo of his daughter very intimately entwined in the arms of their general manager stared up at them. "This was taken in *this* hotel."

"Would you prefer if it had been a competitor's hotel?" She smiled, trying for levity. "Darling, the photograph isn't that terrible."

"She looks—"

"She looks like a young woman kissing the man she's in love with." She rose from her seat and stepped behind him, leaning her head down onto his. "What bothers you more? The fact that this somehow found its way to the papers, or the fact that your daughter is no longer a little girl?"

"He's groping her."

"Oh for heaven's sake. His arms are around her." She slid her arms around his shoulders. "Hers are around him. It happens. Unfortunately, with this family of ours, some of these things tend to feed some foolish public curiosity. You need to go and talk to her."

"Shall I take a copy of the paper with me?"

"Forget the paper." She reached over him and pushed it right off the table. "You heard her last night. She needs to know that she's not a disappointment to you, Mori."

"Kimiko has no desire to hear what I think."

"She knows what you *think*. What she needs to know is what you *feel*. She needs to hear that you love her."

He grimaced. "She's a bright girl. She should know."

"She's an adult, and it doesn't hurt to say the words!"

"Are you going to argue with me over Kimiko?"

"It wouldn't be the first time."

He exhaled noisily and pulled her around to sit on his lap. "What are we going to do about this business between them?"

"Between Kimi and Greg?" Helen toyed with the lapel of his robe. It would be hours yet before the family was to get together for a casual lunch. "That's something that they'll have to work out between them. Greg is a good man. I know you think so, too, if you'll get past thinking your daughter is still ten years old."

"But he *is* too old for her."

"She obviously doesn't think so." She rubbed her fingertips along his collarbone. "You can't fix everything for your children, Mori."

He caught her fingertips and pressed his lips to them, smiling wryly. "As if you have not done your own *fixing*, when it comes to everyone you care about?"

She tucked her tongue between her teeth for a moment. "All right. Perhaps I have."

His eyes narrowed. "You did not send her here with this outcome in mind, did you?"

"Of course not!" She frowned. "I was as shocked as you were when she told us she wanted to work rather than go to school. But I believed working here would be good experience for her. That Greg would see to it that she was given a fair chance at proving herself. Not for our sakes, but for her own. He is a decent man, Mori. He's notoriously private, but I know how far he's taken himself."

"Not unlike someone else we know." He slid his hand through her hair, and she still had to brace herself for the effect he had on her. "You brought yourself far in this world, too, wife of mine."

"Let's just be glad that maybe Kimi hasn't wasted as much time as I did figuring out what she really wants in life."

"Your time was never a waste."

"I know. It brought me George's boys, after a fashion." Her hand slid behind his neck. "It brought you. And Kimi."

He tucked her head against his throat. "I will go and talk with her."

"Good." She slid the knot in his robe free. "After a while."

His mouth hovered over hers. "Merry Christmas, Mrs. Taka."

"Merry Christmas, Mori."

Chapter Thirteen

"I want to know who leaked that picture to the papers, Shin." Greg's voice woke Kimi. "It was obviously clipped from the tape before you stopped it."

She pushed her hair out of her eyes and looked over her shoulder. Greg, wearing nothing but jeans, was standing at the window, looking out at the gray day, his phone in one hand, a rolled newspaper in the other. With the freedom of being behind his back, she looked her fill at *his* behind.

Only, as if he sensed her attention, he turned around and caught her ogling him. His eyebrow peaked.

She hurriedly looked away and scrambled off the bed, pulling her twisted dress back down to her knees where it belonged. The clock on his nightstand told her it was long past the hour when she was supposed to meet the family for lunch. It was obvious that Greg had been awake for a while. There was a room service tray on the desk, as well as a fresh pile of newspapers. Which, from the sound of his conversation, was causing no small amount of consternation.

"I don't care who you have to bribe. Find out. And call me." He snapped his phone shut and tossed it on the desk.

"You must be feeling better." She picked the comforter off the floor and piled it on the foot of the bed. "You sound like your usual self again."

"What'd I tell you about gossip?" He snapped open the newspaper and held it out to her.

She gingerly took it, only to suck in her breath at the small photograph capturing her and Greg that night in the corridor. "Kimiko Taka is the welcoming touch at Taka's new Kyoto branch," she read the caption. "Lovely." She crumpled the page. "I suppose it is too much to hope the photo stayed just in this local paper."

"What do you think?"

She scraped back her hair. "But you got the tape from that night. You said the two security guards with Shin could be trusted."

"I said Shin warned them to stay quiet."

"Well, obviously, they did not heed his warning. Unless Shin—"

"No."

She exhaled. "Are you certain? It is appalling what some papers will pay for a photograph—"

"I said it wasn't Shin."

She subsided. "Fine." She rifled through the rest of the papers. "At least the clip didn't make it above the fold. Given the way people read these days, it will not be noticed by more than half the readers."

"Glad you can be so blasé about it, Kimi."

She lifted her hands. "What would you prefer? The photo could have been worse. It was obviously taken before... before—"

"I started to pull off your dress?" He grimaced. "We'll issue a release that you and I are getting married."

Her heart jumped up into her throat and she actually felt herself sway. *"What?"*

"You heard me. Handy that Jenny is here right now. She can draft the press release."

"Married?"

"We won't have to go through with it. We just keep the press resulting from the photo from making more of the situation than it is."

Her heart plunged right back down to the depths of her soul. She had to brace her arms against the desk because she felt so dizzy. "No, I suppose we must never have that."

"What's wrong?"

"Nothing." She managed to straighten. "I need to get cleaned up. My family expected me an hour ago for lunch." Without looking at him, she headed through to her own room.

He followed, though, and she could only think ironically of all the times she had wished for him to come through the doorway and he had not. Now, when she wished for distance, he gave her none.

"I want to shower, Greg."

He did not budge. "Your parents have undoubtedly seen the photo, too."

"My father reads about ten newspapers a day. So, yes, he probably has." She yanked open drawers, emerging with fresh lingerie, jeans and a sweater. "Rest assured, he is used to my shocking displays." She brushed past him, only to realize that he did still feel hot. "Do you still have a fever?" She pressed her palm to his forehead.

He closed his hands around her wrist and pulled her hand away. "I'm fine."

"Then please excuse me," she said, and slipped beyond him into the bathroom where she closed the door pretty much in his face.

Shaking, she dropped her clothes and quickly turned on the

shower. It had not even begun to steam up the room, as she usually preferred, before she stripped off and stepped under the needle-fine spray.

When she emerged, scrubbed and dressed with her wet hair pinned back in an untidy knot, her room was thankfully empty. There was no sound from Greg's room, either, and she peeked through the doorway.

He was gone, as was the room service tray and most of the newspapers.

She pulled on her low-heeled boots, jammed a knitted stocking cap over her wet head and left her room. But when she went up to her parents' suite, it was empty. So back down the elevator she went. Not surprisingly, she found Greg in his office.

What did surprise her was that her father, Helen and Jenny were there, as well.

"You have been busy," she told Greg, interrupting them. They turned to look at her, but she was focused on Greg. "I was not in the shower very long, but I see you still managed to gather the masses. Has he already told you of his ridiculous plan?"

"What is ridiculous about it?" Mori asked.

She gave him an astonished look. "Papa, even you have to admit that issuing a release that he and I are to be married is completely unnecessary!"

"What is unnecessary about saving your reputation?"

She flopped her hands. "It was a picture of us kissing, not engaging in an orgy!"

Jenny covered her mouth, trying to muffle her laugh. "Sorry," she said. "But I happen to agree with Kimi. Acknowledging the photo just gives more power to it. This family has weathered far more inflammatory scandals than this."

"True enough." Helen sounded amazingly practical, considering that she had endured more than her fair share of unflat tering publicity. First as the trophy wife of George Hanson, then as his widow, and even when the truth about her giving up Jenny as a baby had come out.

"The caption smears her reputation." Greg looked as if his teeth were clenched.

"There was a time when you believed I had no reputation to smear," Kimi reminded him. How well he knew better now, though. "If I do not care what it says, why should you? You're not even identified in the photo. *Your* precious reputation is still intact."

Anger coursed through him. "This isn't about me."

"Isn't it?" Her voice was cool.

The phone on his desk beeped, and he snatched it up. "Sherman," he barked. He listened for a moment. "Keep him there. I'll be up in a sec." He hung up. "Shin has the guard who's admitted leaking the photo. I'll return in a moment. Draft the release," he ordered Jenny before leaving the office.

Helen grabbed Mori's arm, stopping him when he went to follow. "This is Greg's party," she reminded him.

He grimaced, but subsided. He looked at Kimi. "Do you have anything to say?"

"Mori," Helen chided. "What did we talk about this morning?"

He grimaced again. "You say you love the man, Kimi. I come to your room this morning to talk to you, and he tells me you are asleep in *his* room. And now you say you do not wish to marry him?"

Her father knew she had been in Greg's bed? "He has not asked me!" She felt as if she had fallen down the rabbit hole somewhere. "A press release about a marriage that will never happen is *not* a marriage proposal."

"She's right, Mori," Helen said.

Mori looked unconvinced. "Who said it will never happen? Maybe a marriage is exactly the right thing."

"Greg said it!" She stared around the office and realized that

Bridget had appeared at her desk outside his office and was staring at them all, her mouth agape. "And you cannot *arrange* us into anything no matter how convenient you might find it. I have work to do." She did not have, really. She was not scheduled to work that day at all. But any excuse was better than sticking around entertaining ideas of madness. "I will see you later." She strode out of the office. "Merry Christmas, Bridget."

"Merry Christmas, Kimi." Bridget's bemused voice followed her down the hall.

It was a small mercy that Kimi did not encounter anyone else before she made it to the sales department. There, however, she came face-to-face with Charity, who was hunched over an item on her desk.

As soon as Kimi reached her own desk, she could see what that item was.

The newspaper.

"Well." Charity eyed her. "It's a toss-up who's benefiting more from your job here. You or Greg Sherman."

"Shut up, Charity."

"Why? Are you going to run crying to your lover that someone has the nerve to see you for what you are?"

Kimi sighed. She would have cried if it would have made her feel better. "Maybe I should. Or maybe I should tell my parents that you have been unkind. They could ax you from the payroll just as swiftly. Would that satisfy your low expectations then, Charity?"

The other woman's eyes narrowed. "You're spoiled, and you don't have to work for anything you want in this world. All you have to do is bat your eyes and hold out your hand, and you get everything that you want."

"That's enough, Charity." Grace stood in the doorway, looking furious.

Charity flushed.

"Pack your desk and clear out."

"Don't fire her on my account," Kimi said.

"We're not." Greg and Shin appeared behind Grace, at which point Charity managed to look a little nervous.

Shin stepped over behind Charity. "If you have any personal belongings, now is the time to collect them."

"This is insulting."

"What is insulting is bringing you here to the Taka and having you turn on us by delivering that clip your little boyfriend copied to the paparazzi," Grace said.

Stunned, Kimi stared at Charity. *She* had been involved in the leak? "I don't care what you think about me," Kimi told her, "but what have you got against Greg and the hotel?"

"I needed the money, all right?" Charity began haphazardly shoving things from her desk into her purse.

"For what?" Kimi handed her a box of tissues.

Charity snatched one and noisily blew her nose. "For my sister. The one *he* dumped when he came to work for *your* parents."

Greg stepped forward. "What the hell are you talking about?"

Charity blindly pushed a coffee mug into her purse. *"Gretchen?* I suppose you can hardly remember her when you've got Kimi here to keep you busy."

"Wait a minute. Gretchen Bloom from Düsseldorf? She's your sister?"

"Yes." She tried to push a picture frame into her purse, too, but it wouldn't go.

"Gretchen was my head housekeeper," Greg said. "That's all. I never get involved with my staff."

Kimi winced.

"My sister says otherwise."

"Then she's lying," Greg said flatly. "And I'm not interested in why you'd need money for her so badly that you'd sell that clip. Be glad that Shin is just going to escort you from the building and not take you to the authorities."

"Wait." Kimi lifted her hand. *"I* want to know why."

"Damn it, Kimi, I said there was nothing between her sister and me."

"And I believe you!" She eyed Charity. "But what made you so desperate?"

"She's got breast cancer, okay? After Greg left, the new GM made a lot of staff changes, and she lost her job."

"She's probably lying about that, too," Shin warned. "Have you gotten all of your belongings, or not?"

"Where is Gretchen now, Charity?" Kimi asked.

"Living here with me," Charity said grudgingly. "I'm trying to get together enough money to send her back home to the States. There's a program she qualifies for that will get her treatment."

Kimi sighed. "Why didn't you just say so?"

"Why would you care?"

"Why would I not? You know, my family's company has employee assistance funds, Charity. We could have found a way to help you if you would have just spoken up."

"Instead, you sold off something you had no business selling," Greg concluded flatly. "No better than if you had stolen something from a guestroom."

"I would never—"

"Tell it to someone else. Shin, get her out of here."

Kimi bit her lip, watching silently as Shin and Grace escorted Charity out of the office. "She needed help, Greg," she said once they were gone.

"How can you have sympathy for her?"

"Because I believe she wouldn't have stooped to such behavior if she had thought she had another option. She has too much pride." And she knew a little bit about that.

He looked grim. "I never thought I'd accuse you of naïveté. Whatever her reasons, it doesn't change the situation. The photograph is out there. Now we have to deal with it."

"By your fictitious marriage idea?" She shook her head. "No, thank you."

"Why the hell not? On Christmas, you didn't seem to think the notion was that terrible when you said your family could be mine, if I wanted."

"I cannot believe that for an intelligent man you can be so incredibly obtuse."

"I'm trying to protect you, damn it!"

"Why?" Her voice rose, matching his. "I never asked for your protection! The only thing I wanted was your love!"

"Ahem." Grace had returned and was looking awkward. "We can hear you two all the way down the hall."

Kimi snatched up the picture frame that Charity had been unable to fit into her purse. "Don't worry," she assured. "I am leaving, anyway."

"Where are you going?"

"Away from here," she said, and walked out the door.

"Go after her," Grace said in the quiet left by Kimi's exit.

"And make the situation even more complicated?"

"You love her, don't you?"

He jerked. "Whether I do or not is immaterial."

Grace sighed noisily. "You always have been too stubborn for your own good." She flopped her arms. "Well, fine. It's your own grave you're digging. *I* am going home to enjoy the holiday a little longer with my husband." She headed out the door, much the way Kimi had.

Greg realized he was rubbing the hollow spot in his chest and dropped his hand.

As far as he knew, Helen, Mori and Jenny were still waiting in his office, and he headed back in that direction. If there was going to be one small mercy that day, Jenny would have finished the press release he'd asked for.

Then maybe he could figure out how to deal with Kimi.

But when he reached his office, only Helen and Mori remained. Jenny, it seemed, had gone back to her suite. And Kimi, he learned, had not just walked out of the sales department but had left the hotel entirely. "What do you mean, she's gone?" He stared at Mori.

"She was heading to Kyoto Station. She phoned to let us know she would not be returning until the New Year's Eve gala."

Greg sat down, hard, in the chair behind his desk. He looked Mori in the face. "This is my responsibility," he said evenly. "If you want me out of here right now, I won't blame you. I'd planned to wait until after the gala to resign. But Carter can handle things well enough until you can replace me. Grace has every detail for the gala under her thumb."

"Resign?" Helen looked appalled. "What for?"

"Surely you'd be more comfortable with someone else heading this house." His teeth were on edge. "I took advantage of your daughter. While she worked here."

Mori looked pained. "I suspect my daughter is as capable of taking advantage of you. Could we leave Kimiko out of this for the moment?"

"It was difficult enough talking you into leaving your last position," Helen added. "Are you unhappy here, Greg? We haven't filled the Chicago position yet. Perhaps you would be interested in returning to the States."

He stared at them. "I can't leave Kimi out of this." The idea was impossible. Yet they were talking about luring him with a transfer to Chicago if that's what it took to keep him happy?

"Why not?"

"Because I—" He broke off. Saw the satisfaction in Helen's green gaze. "I love her," he admitted gruffly.

Mori's lips tightened slightly. "She will be back for the gala," he said after a moment. "Maybe by then you will feel less unhappy about that fact before you tell *her*."

"Where's she going?"

"To stay with my parents in Nesutotaka."

Greg sat back in his chair. "You're kidding." Just as quickly, he sat forward. "I'll go after her."

"No." Helen spoke up. "Let her be for now, Greg. She's going there to think in peace." Her gaze slipped to her husband. "Like a few others have done before her. Don't worry. She'll return."

"I was surprised also," Mori admitted. "She never liked the village where I grew up. Despite the house I have there, which is more than comfortable. Some day we will travel there together."

Greg stared at them. "You're supposed to be furious. Tell me I'm crazy. Tell me to stay away from her."

"Would that do any good?" Mori asked. "I saw the way you looked at her. The way you stood up for her. As my wife reminds me, some things are not for me to decide. Resolve in yourself what is to be, Greg. Your position with Taka is perfectly secure as long as you want, no matter what happens."

"Working here is not turning out as I expected at all," Greg muttered. Kimi had tried to tell him, but he hadn't wanted to listen. It was so much easier sticking with the world that you knew. That you expected.

"Well," Helen said, smiling, "nothing is ever quite as expected when it comes to our family. Now is as good a time as any to get used to it."

But Greg had the feeling that getting used to anything about the Takas was going to take considerably longer than an afternoon or two.

By the time the night of the gala rolled around, he'd had cause to reaffirm that particular belief as the rest of the Hanson clan arrived in the form of David and Nina Hanson and their brood, which—judging by the swell of Nina's abdomen—was going to be increasing in size pretty soon.

Then there were the other priority arrivals. The corporate suits who, along with Mori and Helen, were the backbone of getting the hospitality division off the ground. The architects. Designers. Bankers. Even a handful of celebrities.

Greg worked his way around the grand ballroom, welcoming them all to the gala. But he still couldn't see the one person he was watching for.

"Don't worry," Jenny said, approaching him after he'd spoken with one of the crowned royals there that evening and watched the man and his wife move off with Mori and Helen to the dance floor that was swollen with ball gowns and tuxedos. Jenny wore a narrow black gown and a choker of diamonds, and she'd spent plenty of time on the dance floor with Richard. "Kimi will be here."

He hated the idea of being that transparent. "Most of the guests have already arrived by now." Still there was no sign of her dark head.

It had been nearly a week since he'd seen her. Talked to her. Touched her. A week that had felt like a bloody year. "She's going to miss the children's orchestra playing if she's much later. They go on right before midnight."

"She'll be here," Jenny assured again.

When Kimi was, *if* she was, he knew it was no guarantee that she would want to stay. Not after the gala. Not with him. Not after everything that had happened.

"I should have gone after her."

"She needed some time, Greg. Stop worrying. Mori went to see her. Even he said she is all right." She patted his shoulder before moving off to greet someone else she obviously knew.

Not worry? Easier said than done. Particularly when his position as general manager forced him to introduce the children's orchestra who had taken the stage temporarily vacated by the professional orchestra that Grace had contracted.

Stepping aside when they began to play, his gaze scanned the crowd, but it was futile.

She'd changed her mind. Just as he'd expected.

The children's orchestra played only a few songs, but it was still enough, he knew, to sway the hearts of many who were there into opening their purse strings with contributions. He supposed if there was nothing else that he'd done right, at least there was this.

Once the children were off the stage again, he headed into the crowd. There was only minutes before the New Year rang in. In Japan, the ringing was more than a phrase, as the old year was ushered out with the ringing of temple bells. One hundred and eight times to atone for the same number of humankind's evil passions.

Maybe by the time the last gong had rung, even Greg would feel some ease.

His throat ached, and this time it had nothing whatsoever to do with the bug that had bitten him over Christmas.

He turned away from the crowded dance floor, making his way around the perimeter of the room, past the buffet tables that had been replenished several times over since the first guests had arrived hours earlier. He took the service elevator down to the lobby.

There, it was almost painfully quiet. The water in the fountain gurgled softly. The two young women manning reception smiled at him as he walked past them. "It's midnight, Mr. Sherman. Happy New Year!"

"You, too, ladies." He headed toward the front door, only to stop short at the sight of Johnny ushering Yukio Taka and his wife inside the building. That was surprising enough. But what stopped his heart for a moment was the sight of Kimi following behind them.

She wore a scarlet kimono-style gown. It was not exactly traditional. Nor was it quite modern, either. Her hair was a long, shining sheaf draped over her shoulder.

And she started his heart again when her dark gaze met his.

It was all he could do to properly greet her grandparents.

"I talked my grandparents into coming to the grand opening," Kimi finally said after the proprieties had been observed. "It took somewhat longer than I expected to get here."

"I will show you to the ballroom," Greg offered to the

couple. Thankfully, Yukio waved him off with a gesture barely shy of impatience and headed toward the elevators with his beaming wife hurrying alongside him.

"My grandmother despaired of my grandfather agreeing to be here tonight," Kimi said as they left. "Even after all this time he resists the changes my father has brought to the family."

"I wish you hadn't disappeared," he said bluntly.

Her lashes swept down. "*Sumimasen. I wanted time. To think." She made a face, thoroughly modern Kimi. "Who would have thought I would do that so well in Nesutotaka?"

"Maybe you're more in tune with your Japanese heritage than you thought."

She touched her gown. "Maybe."

Johnny opened the door again for another guest and from outside, they could hear the faint, throaty peal of a distant bell.

"The bells have been ringing for a while." He pushed his hand into his pocket to keep from reaching for her.

"*Joya no Kane.* My father used to take me to a temple in Tokyo to hear them." She moistened her lips. "I have seen Charity. I arranged for her and her sister to get back to the States."

"She won't ever work for a Taka hotel again."

"I know. Maybe I just felt that if I hadn't been so focused on the way people were treating me, I might have noticed now troubled she was."

"You're more forgiving than I am."

"You didn't issue your press release about the photograph."

"Jenny's opinion prevailed."

"She is smart that way." She looked away, and a lock of her hair slid over her arm. "I have decided to go back to the U.S., too. Chicago. I'm going to start my MBA."

The pain was swift and lasting, like a kick to the gut. "Good for you," he managed. "Have you told your parents this time?"

"Yes." Her smile was wry but painfully brief. "They are pleased."

The elevator chimed, and several laughing couples exited, heading across the lobby floor. Again Greg could hear the bell tolling when Johnny ushered them out.

"And after that, then what?"

"If my father is smart, he will want me to work for him. If he is not so smart, I will work for others."

He believed her. "In the States."

"In the States. Or elsewhere." She looked away. "I should get to the ballroom before my family decides I have deserted them entirely."

"They all knew you would come." He was the one who had doubted.

She had returned, though. Just not to him.

"Excuse me." She started for the elevators. The guest elevators. He knew the move was not unintentional.

She was a Taka. She was not staff. He was.

That was not ever going to change.

Which meant, if he didn't want to lose her, he'd have to do the changing.

"Kimi, wait. Don't go."

She paused, but didn't turn. "To the ballroom?"

"To Chicago."

She slowly looked back at him over her shoulder. There were tears in her eyes. "Do not ask me to stay at the beginning of this year if you do not intend to be with me at the end of it."

He went to her and took her hands. "I will be with you at the end of fifty years."

She looked up at him. "Why have you changed your mind now?"

"Because the past week has been about the most damned bleak time in my life."

"I am sorry. Is that the only reason?"

He didn't know why the words were still so hard to say. "I love you, all right?"

A tear slipped from the corner of her eye.

He caught it with his thumb. "I love you," he repeated more gently.

Another tear slid free.

He cupped her nape and pressed his lips to her eyes. "I love you," he whispered. And he realized it wasn't difficult at all. "Don't be sorry. Don't be unhappy. Just tell me I haven't lost you for good."

"You are not worried some will think you are with me because of your career?"

"I stopped caring what anyone else but you thought when you walked away from me. Your parents were...are...something else."

"I told you they would not care about what happens between us."

Somewhere behind them, the elevators disgorged another group of noisy New Year's celebrants. "They care, all right," he assured her. "Amazingly, they don't seem to hold it against me."

"They, too, wish for me to be happy. Even my father convinced me of that when he came to see me in Nesutotaka."

He realized with some surprise that his hands were shaking. He ran them down to her shoulders. "And what will make you happy, Kimiko?"

"Fifty years," she whispered. "Or longer."

Relief, deeper and unlike anything he had ever known, slid through his veins. He pulled her close. "You will still get your MBA. I'll go with you to Chicago, if I have to."

"We need not go anywhere. I can do it from here." Her voice was muffled against the shoulder of his tuxedo.

He pulled her back, to look into her face. "You're willing to stay in Japan?"

Kimi looked up into his eyes and saw at last everything she had ever dared to hope for. Love. Trust. A future.

With him.

"Japan or anywhere else that you are." Finally she felt no hesitation. No uncertainty. She *was* a Taka.

He still looked as if he was not quite ready to believe. "And you *will* marry me? Have kids, argue over the remote—all of that?"

Her heart squeezed. Oh, there would be so much to share with this man. "Only if Anton Tessier can coordinate the wedding."

He stilled, looking abruptly appalled. "If that's what'll make you happy."

She laughed softly. "I am kidding." She slid her hand behind his neck, pulling his head down to hers. "Yes, I will marry you. And *all* of that. And I wish to meet your mother, who will tell me what herbs to keep on hand should you become too aged and infirm for my liking."

"I can tell you right now that isn't likely to be a problem." He fervently covered her mouth with his.

With her heart seeming ready to burst out of her kimono, Kimi finally dragged back her head to draw in a gasp of air. She was vaguely aware of the small, formally attired crowd they seemed to be drawing. "Mr. Sherman, we are in the middle of the hotel lobby. What will people say?"

His laughter suddenly rang through the lobby as he lifted her in a slow circle. "Let 'em talk. They'll all be saying, 'Look at him. He's the luckiest man in the world.'"

She pressed her hand to his jaw. Looked into those stained-glass eyes and knew that she was the luckiest woman because this New Year was just the beginning of a lifetime of them.

"Happy New Year, Mr. Sherman. I love you."

"Happy New Year, Ms. Taka. I love you."

* * * * *

Silhouette Desire kicks off 2009 with
MAN OF THE MONTH,
*a yearlong program featuring
incredible heroes by stellar authors.*

When navy SEAL Hunter Cabot returns home for some
much-needed R & R, he discovers he's a married man.
There's just one problem: he's never met his "bride."

*Enjoy this sneak peek at Maureen Child's
AN OFFICER AND A MILLIONAIRE.
Available January 2009
from Silhouette Desire.*

One

Hunter Cabot, Navy SEAL, had a healing bullet wound in his side, thirty days' leave and, apparently, a wife he'd never met.

On the drive into his hometown of Springville, California, he stopped for gas at Charlie Evans's service station. That's where the trouble started.

"Hunter! Man, it's good to see you! Margie didn't tell us you were coming home."

"Margie?" Hunter leaned back against the front fender of his black pickup truck and winced as his side gave a small twinge of pain. Silently then, he watched as the man he'd known since high school filled his tank.

Charlie grinned, shook his head and pumped gas. "Guess your wife was lookin' for a little 'alone' time with you, huh?"

"My—" Hunter couldn't even say the word. *Wife?* He didn't have a wife. "Look, Charlie..."

"Don't blame her, of course," his friend said with a wink as he finished up and put the gas cap back on. "You being gone all the time with the SEALs must be hard on the ol' love life."

He'd never had any complaints, Hunter thought, frowning at the man still talking a mile a minute. "What're you—"

"Bet Margie's anxious to see you. She told us all about that R & R trip you two took to Bali." Charlie's dark brown eyebrows lifted and wiggled.

"Charlie..."

"Hey, it's okay, you don't have to say a thing, man."

What the hell could he say? Hunter shook his head, paid for his gas and as he left, told himself Charlie was just losing it. Maybe the guy had been smelling gas fumes too long.

But as it turned out, it wasn't just Charlie. Stopped at a red light on Main Street, Hunter glanced out his window to smile at Mrs. Harker, his second-grade teacher who was now at least a hundred years old. In the middle of the crosswalk, the old lady stopped and shouted, "Hunter Cabot, you've got yourself a wonderful wife. I hope you appreciate her."

Scowling now, he only nodded at the old woman—the only teacher who'd ever scared the crap out of him. What the hell was going on here? Was everyone but him nuts?

His temper beginning to boil, he put up with a few more comments about his "wife" on the drive through town before finally pulling into the wide, circular drive leading to the Cabot mansion. Hunter didn't have a clue what was going on, but he planned to get to the bottom of it. Fast.

He grabbed his duffel bag, stalked into the house and paid no attention to the housekeeper, who ran at him, fluttering both hands. "Mr. Hunter!"

"Sorry, Sophie," he called out over his shoulder as he took the stairs two at a time. "Need a shower, then we'll talk."

He marched down the long, carpeted hallway to the rooms that were always kept ready for him. In his suite, Hunter tossed the duffel down and stopped dead. The shower in his bathroom was running. His *wife?*

Anger and curiosity boiled in his gut, creating a churning mass that had him moving forward without even thinking about it. He opened the bathroom door to a wall of steam and the sound of a woman singing—off-key. Margie, no doubt.

Well, if she was his wife... Hunter walked across the room, yanked the shower door open and stared in at a curvy, naked, temptingly wet woman.

She whirled to face him, slapping her arms across her naked body while she gave a short, terrified scream.

Hunter smiled. "Hi, honey. I'm home."

* * * * *

Be sure to look for
AN OFFICER AND A MILLIONAIRE
by USA TODAY *bestselling author Maureen Child.*
Available January 2009 from Silhouette Desire.

CELEBRATE
60 YEARS
OF PURE READING PLEASURE
WITH HARLEQUIN®!

We'll be spotlighting a different series
every month throughout 2009
to celebrate our 60th anniversary.
Look for Silhouette Desire® in January!

Collect all 12 books in the Silhouette Desire®
Man of the Month continuity, starting in
January 2009 with *An Officer and a Millionaire*
by *USA TODAY* bestselling author
Maureen Child.

*Look for one new Man of the Month title
every month in 2009!*

✦ Silhouette®

SPECIAL EDITION™

USA TODAY bestselling author
MARIE FERRARELLA

FORTUNES OF TEXAS: RETURN TO RED ROCK

PLAIN JANE AND THE PLAYBOY

To kill time at a New Year's party, playboy Jorge Mendoza shows the host's teenage son how to woo the ladies. The random target of Jorge's charms: wallflower Jane Gilliam. But with one kiss at midnight, introverted Jane turns the tables on this would-be Casanova, as the commitment-phobe falls for her hook, line and sinker!

*Available January 2009
wherever you buy books.*

REQUEST YOUR FREE BOOKS!
2 FREE NOVELS PLUS 2 FREE GIFTS!

SPECIAL EDITION®
Life, Love and Family!

YES! Please send me 2 FREE Silhouette Special Edition® novels and my 2 FREE gifts (gifts are worth about $10). After receiving them, if I don't wish to receive any more books, I can return the shipping statement marked "cancel." If I don't cancel, I will receive 6 brand-new novels every month and be billed just $4.24 per book in the U.S. or $4.99 per book in Canada, plus 25¢ shipping and handling per book and applicable taxes, if any*. That's a savings of at least 15% off the cover price! I understand that accepting the 2 free books and gifts places me under no obligation to buy anything. I can always return a shipment and cancel at any time. Even if I never buy another book from Silhouette, the two free books and gifts are mine to keep forever.

235 SDN EEYU   335 SDN EEY6

Name	(PLEASE PRINT)	
Address		Apt. #
City	State/Prov.	Zip/Postal Code

Signature (if under 18, a parent or guardian must sign)

Mail to the **Silhouette Reader Service:**
IN U.S.A.: P.O. Box 1867, Buffalo, NY 14240-1867
IN CANADA: P.O. Box 609, Fort Erie, Ontario L2A 5X3

Not valid to current subscribers of Silhouette Special Edition books.

Want to try two free books from another line?
Call 1-800-873-8635 or visit www.morefreebooks.com.

* Terms and prices subject to change without notice. N.Y. residents add applicable sales tax. Canadian residents will be charged applicable provincial taxes and GST. Offer not valid in Quebec. This offer is limited to one order per household. All orders subject to approval. Credit or debit balances in a customer's account(s) may be offset by any other outstanding balance owed by or to the customer. Please allow 4 to 6 weeks for delivery. Offer available while quantities last.

Your Privacy: Silhouette is committed to protecting your privacy. Our Privacy Policy is available online at www.eHarlequin.com or upon request from the Reader Service. From time to time we make our lists of customers available to reputable third parties who may have a product or service of interest to you. If you would prefer we not share your name and address, please check here. ☐

SSE08R

New York Times **Bestselling Author**

SHERRYL WOODS

When Jeanette Brioche helped to launch The Corner Spa, she found more than professional satisfaction—she discovered deep friendships. But even the Sweet Magnolias can't persuade her that the holidays are anything more than misery.

Pushed into working on the town's Christmas festival, Jeanette teams up with the sexy new town manager. Tom McDonald may be the only person in Serenity who's less enthused about family and the holidays than she is.

But with romance in the air, Jeanette and Tom discover that this just may be a season of miracles, after all.

Welcome to Serenity

The Sweet Magnolias

*Available the first week
of December 2008
wherever paperbacks
are sold!*

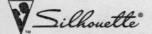

COMING NEXT MONTH

#1945 THE STRANGER AND TESSA JONES—
Christine Rimmer
Bravo Family Ties
The Bravos meet the Jones Gang as two of Christine Rimmer's famous Special Edition families come together in one very special book. Snowed in with an amnesiac stranger during a freak blizzard, Tessa Jones soon finds out her guest is none other than heartbreaker Ash Bravo. And that's when things really heat up....

#1946 PLAIN JANE AND THE PLAYBOY—Marie Ferrarella
Fortunes of Texas: Return to Red Rock
To kill time at a New Year's party, playboy Jorge Mendoza shows the host's teenage son how to woo the ladies. The random target of Jorge's charms: wallflower Jane Gilliam. But with one kiss at midnight, introverted Jane turns the tables on this would-be Casanova, as the commitment-phobe falls for her hook, line and sinker!

#1947 COWBOY TO THE RESCUE—Stella Bagwell
Men of the West
Hired to investigate the mysterious death of the Sandbur Ranch matriarch's late husband, private investigator Christina Logan enlists the help of cowboy-to-the-core Lex Saddler, Sandbur's youngest—and singlest—scion. Together, they find the truth...and each other.

#1948 REINING IN THE RANCHER—Karen Templeton
Wed in the West
Horse breeder Johnny Griego is blindsided by the news—both his ex-girlfriend Thea Benedict *and* his teenage daughter are pregnant. Never one to shirk responsibility, Johnny does the right thing and proposes to Thea. But Thea wants happily-ever-after, not a mere marriage of convenience. Can she rein in the rancher enough to have both?

#1949 SINGLE MOM SEEKS...—Teresa Hill
All newly divorced Lily Tanner wants is a safe, happy life with her two adorable daughters. Until hunky FBI agent Nick Malone moves in next door with his orphaned nephew. Now the pretty single mom's single days just might be numbered....

#1950 I STILL DO—Christie Ridgway
During a chance reunion in Vegas, former childhood sweethearts Will Dailey and Emily Garner let loose a little and make good on an old pledge—to wed each other if they weren't otherwise taken by age thirty! But in the cold light of day, the firefighter and librarian's quickie marriage doesn't seem like such a bright idea. Would their whim last a lifetime?

SSECNM1208BPA